*"I can resist anything. I have incredible willpower."*

"You don't get tempted? Ever?" She peeled back the paper wrapper with her perfectly manicured fingertips and took a bite of the muffin. She closed her eyes as sheer bliss bloomed on her face. "Mmm. This is so good. Apple cinnamon. It's like a sugary hug." Her eyes slowly drifted open and she licked her lower lip.

Suddenly Grey was thinking too much about temptation and Autumn's mouth.

Even though they were technically in a business meeting, the thought did cross his mind that he wouldn't mind taking off her glasses and digging his hand into her hair, curling his fingertips into her nape and kissing her.

It was a purely carnal thought, with no emotion attached. Grey didn't believe in romance. But he did believe in sex.

"I'll take your word for it."

\* \* \*

*Best Laid Wedding Plans* by Karen Booth is part of the Moonlight Ridge series.

Dear Reader,

I'm thrilled to introduce my contribution to the Moonlight Ridge series! This collaboration with two of my best author friends, Joss Wood and Reese Ryan, was born at the 2019 Romance Writers of America conference in New York. Between drinks, meals out, long conversations and dancing for hours at the Harlequin party, we became nearly inseparable. We talked about how much we've loved collaborating on other Harlequin Desire series like Secrets of the A-List and Texas Cattleman's Club. And that's what got us thinking...

So we came up with the Holloway family—Mack, Grey and Travis, along with patriarch Jameson. We wanted three heroes with different backgrounds, so we made them foster brothers. It worked well because Jameson, their adoptive father, has a huge heart. We set the series in beautiful Asheville, NC, because it made a lovely backdrop for these three very different heroes to return home, face the obstacles of their shared history and make room for love in their lives.

I hope you love *Best Laid Wedding Plans*. Email me at karen@karenbooth.net and let me know!

*Karen*

# KAREN BOOTH

---

# BEST LAID WEDDING PLANS

HARLEQUIN
DESIRE

# HARLEQUIN®
# DESIRE™

Recycling programs for this product may not exist in your area.

ISBN-13: 978-1-335-73515-7

Best Laid Wedding Plans

Copyright © 2021 by Karen Booth

This edition published by arrangement with Harlequin Books S.A.

For questions and comments about the quality of this book, please contact us at CustomerService@Harlequin.com.

Harlequin Enterprises ULC
22 Adelaide St. West, 40th Floor
Toronto, Ontario M5H 4E3, Canada
www.Harlequin.com

**Printed in U.S.A.**

**Karen Booth** is a Midwestern girl transplanted in the South, raised on '80s music and repeated readings of *Forever* by Judy Blume. When she takes a break from the art of romance, she's listening to music with her college-age kids or sweet-talking her husband into making her a cocktail. Learn more about Karen at karenbooth.net.

## Books by Karen Booth

### Harlequin Desire

*Blue Collar Billionaire*

### *The Sterling Wives*

*Once Forbidden, Twice Tempted*
*High Society Secrets*
*All He Wants for Christmas*

### *Moonlight Ridge*

*Best Laid Wedding Plans*

Visit her Author Profile page at Harlequin.com, or karenbooth.net, for more titles.

You can also find Karen Booth on Facebook, along with other Harlequin Desire authors, at Facebook.com/HarlequinDesireAuthors!

For Joss Wood and Reese Ryan,
my dear friends and Harlequin Desire sisters.
I love you both so much!

# One

Autumn Kincaid prided herself on being optimistic. She took every chance to live in the moment. Unfortunately, it wasn't enough to keep her past from following her. Case in point, that morning's loathsome headline on a gossip website: "Wedding Planner Left at the Altar; Daughter of Controversial Hollywood Producer Humiliated."

She squeezed the steering wheel of her silver BMW as she closed in on the entrance to Moonlight Ridge, the luxury mountain resort in Asheville, NC, where as an independent contractor she arranged all their weddings on a shared profit basis. It had been nearly three months since her fiancé dumped her. This was *not* a breaking story. No, the tabloid had chosen to rehash her sad tale of wedding planner–turned–jilted bride, a story they had covered when it happened, because it gave them an excuse to write about her dad. That meant clicks and dollar signs. Her dad was a powerful disgrace, and a great way for some people to make money. And just like she had for most of her life, Autumn was paying the price.

She sighed as she pulled into a parking space, then climbed out of her car and marched up the walk to the main entrance of the historic inn at Moonlight Ridge. *Inn* was a complete misnomer. It was an inn the way a mansion is also a house. Nearly one hundred years old, it went on for days, with a maze of halls and rooms, all of it elegant and finely appointed with original details like hand-carved stone, exotic woods and marble floors. Autumn loved planning weddings for Moonlight Ridge, but her latest piece of negative publicity put her contract with the luxury resort in serious jeopardy. It was hard enough trying to convince modern brides that slightly outdated Moonlight Ridge was the go-to wedding venue. But that had been changing with recent renovations. She thought her job would get easier—until the tabloids interfered again.

Her stomach soured at the thought of more damage control, but she had to look to the future and deal with her lot in life. So she held her head high, strolled inside and through the lobby, then started up the wide stairs to the third-floor administrative offices to meet with her best friend, Molly Haskell, who was also general manager at the luxury resort.

Despite everything, Autumn could see two bright spots. First, she no longer lived in Los Angeles and she'd been smart enough to never move to New York, where the shock waves of the tabloid story would be impossible to escape. Her adopted home of Asheville was quiet and serene. The people were lovely. She could be relatively anonymous here. That was all she really wanted—to be free. To simply be Autumn, wedding planner. It was a simple ask.

As Autumn stopped in the doorway of the manager's office, her other bright spot came into view—her best friend, and the reason she'd come back to Asheville in the first place—Molly. Even knowing that they were set to discuss Autumn's problems, Autumn felt immense relief knowing Molly was in charge.

Molly glanced up from her desk, holding her phone to her ear. Her normally bright green eyes were clouded with concern. She waved Autumn in, then turned her chair and looked out over the lush mountain view outside her window. June in Asheville was truly lovely, and the trees and budding flowers showed it. Autumn quietly took a seat and patiently waited, even though her leg wouldn't stop bobbing in place.

"I understand. I hope you find another wedding venue," Molly said to the person she was speaking to.

Autumn's stomach lurched. Had another bride canceled? This had happened before, right after the first spate of negative publicity over Autumn being unceremoniously left at the altar. As if a broken heart hadn't been enough, humiliation and professional ruin came along with it.

"Certainly. I'll have the accounting department return your deposit check immediately. Please let us know if you change your mind." Molly whirled around in her chair, hung up the phone and smiled sweetly at Autumn. The distinct aroma of pity was in the air. "How are you doing? Holding up okay?" she asked.

"I was going to say I'm fine, but now I'm not so sure. Was that another cancellation?"

Molly noticeably winced. "I'm afraid so. Blair Morgan. Her mother called and said they were upset about the negative publicity. They also didn't seem to realize who your father is."

The disappointment Autumn felt was immense. She'd worked hard to court Blair and her fiancé, but she'd known all along that she had a very skittish mother-of-the-bride on her hands. "I wish I could say that I'm surprised, but I'm not. I'm just disappointed. And embarrassed."

"I'm so sorry."

"Does Mr. Holloway know about the article this time? I know you were able to keep the first one out of sight." Jameson Holloway was the owner of Moonlight Ridge. He'd been the manager decades ago and it had been willed to him by Tip O'Sullivan, the very appreciative but childless owner of the sprawling estate. Autumn hated the thought of disappointing Jameson. He was a kind and generous man. He also had a reputation to uphold. He was a beloved figure in Asheville.

"I don't think he knows. Mack and I are doing our best to keep any stressful news away from him. That and the cigars out of his mouth."

Autumn managed a quiet laugh. Jameson's love for cigars was well known, but he'd had a brain episode a few months ago, which meant no more smoking. Molly told her a brain episode was another way of saying he narrowly avoided an actual aneurysm. Thankfully, he was reportedly recovering well in his home on the Moonlight Ridge property. Still, everyone was concerned, especially his three adopted sons—Mack, Grey and Travis. The brothers were returning to Asheville from their various homes across the US to look after Moonlight Ridge while Jameson recovered. Mack was up first, with Grey and Travis expected some time over the course of the next several months. It had been a bit of good luck for Molly—she and Mack, sweethearts from when they were young, had fallen back in love. Autumn was happy for her, even when her own romance hadn't played out the way she'd hoped.

"I hope they can keep this whole thing away from Mr. Holloway," Autumn said. "I mean, Jared dumped me three months ago. Isn't it old news?"

Molly got up from her chair and walked around to the front of her desk, crouching down and taking Autumn's hand. She peered up at Autumn with her big green eyes and tucked a few tendrils of her crazy blond curls behind one ear. "It is, and it isn't. I think you're so eager to move on that you forget it's still fresh in some people's minds."

Was that really true? Autumn didn't want to believe so. "I'm a survivor. You know that. I dust myself off and move ahead."

"And I think you're doing great. I know how hard you're trying."

Autumn so appreciated Molly, whom she'd met when

Molly and Autumn were eleven. Autumn's family had traveled from Los Angeles to Asheville for a vacation at Moonlight Ridge. Molly's dad had worked for Jameson and when he died, Jameson allowed the family to live on the property. Molly and Autumn hit it off when Autumn had been walking her family's dog and it got off its leash down by the lake on the property. Molly had helped Autumn track down the pup before her difficult dad found out about it. A friendship was started then, but it got stronger when Autumn's family returned the next summer. When Autumn's family didn't return for a third summer, the girls remained in contact, but it slowly faded as they got older. But they both knew theirs was the type of friendship where no matter the time passed or the distance, once reunited they would instantly be best friends again. The strength of their bond was what made Autumn feel comfortable with the idea of coming to Asheville when things in LA got to be too much.

"Thank you. I appreciate that," Autumn said. "I want you to know that I won't let any more brides bail on us."

Molly bit down on her lower lip and Autumn sensed her hesitation. "Yeah. About that. Mack told me this morning that he thinks the brothers should be more hands-on with the wedding part of the business. At least for a while. Until this blows over and we're on more stable ground. Maybe get a few more bookings."

Autumn had not bargained on this. She'd thought Molly might gently tighten the screws, but the brothers? "What do they know about weddings? Mack owns breweries, Travis is a chef, and the other brother's an architect, isn't he?"

"Yes. Grey's a green architect. He specializes in helping big companies build facilities that are eco-friendly. And I think Grey is who you'd be working with."

"Buildings and bridesmaids. Makes perfect sense." Autumn didn't want to roll her eyes, but this was Molly. She knew Autumn's sense of humor.

"Mack still needs to talk to him about it. He's coming back to Asheville today."

"For how long?"

"The summer. He's adamant about that. He doesn't want to stay any longer than he has to."

Autumn didn't like the sound of Grey Holloway, but what choice did she have? She'd caused problems and she had to try to fix them. "Okay."

"Look. I think this will be good. Grey knows how to run a successful business and he's incredibly good with numbers. He knows a lot of Asheville families from his time living here, so that could come in handy." Molly stood up and returned to her chair.

Autumn wrapped her arms around her waist. It was not the body language of a person who was feeling upbeat, but this was her natural reaction. Everything had been going great until Jared dumped her. He'd seemed perfect for her—a man with big aspirations and dreams who was also grounded and sincere. But their love—and their dream wedding—all fell apart when Jared received a job offer at a big brokerage firm in New York, one with an absurd number of zeroes attached to it. He'd asked Autumn to come with him, but it was a half-hearted request, and that was when she'd first sensed something was wrong. He was worried that the notoriety of her family might damage his new career prospects. He didn't say it in so many words, but his face, and ultimately his actions told her all she needed to know. Autumn only wished he hadn't chosen to make his decision three days before their wedding. Advance notice would've been nice.

Despite the heartbreak, Autumn didn't regret her choice to remain in Asheville. She'd carved out a career for herself here. She had Molly by her side. She felt safe. She wasn't about to turn her back on that, but it did cast doubt on the feelings she'd thought she'd had for Jared. Their relationship had not been built on the strongest foundation. "It's my fault. I fell for the wrong guy."

Molly eagerly nodded. "I know. I'm sorry."

Tears stung Autumn's eyes, but she was not going to cry, not even in front of her best friend. She had to get it together. "It's fine. Jared and I just weren't meant to be." Autumn removed her glasses and polished the lenses with the hem of her blouse. The world around her went fuzzy, so she was quick to put them back on.

"Don't worry. You'll turn everything around, personally and professionally. With Grey's help on the wedding side."

Autumn still wasn't sure about this. "What if I say no? I'm not a Moonlight Ridge employee. I'm an independent contractor. Technically, I work for myself."

Molly twisted her lips, again seeming uncomfortable. "But because we share the profits from these weddings, you'd lose a substantial income. Can you afford to walk away? If I were you, I'd do whatever you can to make the Holloway brothers happy."

"Is my contract in jeopardy?"

"Weddings are a huge source of revenue for the resort, and the brothers are overhauling every aspect of the business right now. They want to know that Jameson's financial future is secure. Plus, if the money side doesn't improve, there might not be a way to save Moonlight Ridge."

"So, that's a yes."

"Let's not think about worst-case scenarios. Focus on showing Grey how hard you work and everything you do to make weddings at Moonlight Ridge the best they can be."

Autumn wasn't convinced, but her inner optimist was willing to try. "Okay. Obviously, I'll do whatever you think I should. I'm not about to give up because of a few bumps in the road. Or a mother-of-the-bride who decides I made her nervous."

"That's the spirit." Molly smiled wide and got up from her desk. Autumn took that as her cue that their informal meeting was over, and rose from her chair as well. "And look on the bright side."

"Bright side?"

Molly gripped Autumn's shoulder, offering some reassurance. "Yes. If it ends up being Grey, he's super hot and single."

"It's not a good idea to get involved with the man who holds my professional life in his hands." It was more than that though, it was her whole future. She'd settled on staying here, she had to make it work.

"Doesn't mean it won't be fun to work with him." A quizzical look crossed Molly's face. "Except, come to think of it, I'm not sure I've ever seen him actually be fun."

*I can't wait to meet him.* "Slow down, Molly. Don't sell the idea of Grey Holloway too hard."

Even though Grey Holloway had recently been back in Asheville, crossing the threshold into his adoptive father Jameson's home was like stepping back in time. "Hello? Mack?" he called into the grand foyer for his brother, who'd asked Grey to meet him.

"Up here," Mack yelled from somewhere up on the second floor.

"On my way," Grey muttered as he strode through the spacious open-plan kitchen and past the dining room to the back staircase. Jameson had lived in this house, a renovated barn on the sprawling grounds of Moonlight Ridge, for years. All around Grey were reminders of his history here—countless framed photographs of him and his brothers dotting the wall, the gleaming wood dining table with chairs lined up like soldiers, and out through the windows, the vistas of rolling hills, lush lawns and thick stands of trees.

Some glimpses of the past were on display for all to see, but still more were tucked inside Grey's head, precious to him as the air he breathed. Like the way Jameson had rescued eight-year-old Grey from his volatile family situation and welcomed him into this loving and stable household. He'd done the same for his adopted brothers Mack and Travis. More than twenty years later, Grey couldn't be more grateful. He was certain Mack and Travis felt the same way.

Some parts of their shared past were less rosy however, like the car accident that drove a wedge between the three brothers. That night in Mack's old truck had been truly terrible, dark and stormy chaos. Tempers were running high and in a moment of recklessness Grey hated to remember, he'd lost his cool and ripped into his brothers. Years of being the calm one—the peacemaker—had caught up with him. He completely let loose, saying ugly things that he wished he could take back. And then Mack misjudged the curve on that old logging road, the three went into the ravine, and their lives were changed forever.

They nearly lost Travis. And Grey vowed that night to never ever lose control again.

The thought made Grey's throat grow tight. Despite the promise he'd made to himself, he might never get over the guilt. Then again, Mack and Travis were no angels. Mack had been the instigator, and Travis…well, they never would've been out there at all if he hadn't been chasing a girl who didn't want him. They might not be biological siblings, or even look alike, but the sheer strength of their bond had made them feel invincible. That night, their love for each other drove them apart. Grey wasn't sure they'd ever be back together like they'd once been, but he and Mack were trying. Travis was a more difficult nut to crack, but he'd also lost the most.

At the top of the stairs were the bedrooms Mack, Travis and Grey had inhabited when they were growing up, none of which looked as they had all those years ago. After a decade of begging the brothers to visit at the same time—to finally reconcile—Jameson made a rather transparent play by gutting and renovating the entire second floor, turning each bedroom into an en suite. *Plenty of room for any of you to bring a girlfriend along,* he'd said. *Or maybe someday, wives and grandchildren.* Jameson would do anything to strip away their excuses. He was as sentimental and softhearted as they came. Stubborn and strong, too. As luck would have it, the renovations made it an easier sell when Mack hired Giada, Jameson's live-in nurse. She'd been a housekeeper at Moonlight Ridge when the boys were young, before she went to nursing school. After several years as an ER nurse in Florida, she was back in Asheville to look after Jameson and was currently living in Mack's old room.

At the end of the hall was Jameson's home study. Light beamed out into the corridor, telling Grey exactly where Mack was. "Does Pops know you're up here, digging around?" Grey inched his way inside. It looked like a tornado had ripped through an office supply factory. There were piles of paper, binders and ledgers everywhere.

"You're back." Mack dropped a banker's file box on Jameson's desk, then walked over to give Grey a hug. "How was your flight from New York?"

Grey clapped Mack on the back. Despite the embrace, it still felt as though there was a wall between them. Would that ever go away? "Fine. I had to transfer in Charlotte, but I got some work done."

"How are the brewery plans coming?" Mack stood back and gave Grey half a smile, his intense eyes glinting.

"I'm nearly done." Grey was currently working on the architectural plans for the brewery Mack planned to put in the abandoned stone barn on the property. Mack had become a true mogul in the beer world over the last decade, with twenty-five locations of his Corkscrew Craft Beer Brewery across the country. Mack had a staff architect, but he'd gone out of his way to ask Grey to design this one. It was an olive branch and Grey had been happy to take it.

"Fantastic. I'm excited to work on this together," Mack said.

"Me too. We should walk the site together and talk through the details. I'm here until Labor Day, so sooner is better." Grey could hardly believe that he was back in Asheville for an extended stay. When he'd left for New York and architecture school more than ten years ago, he'd never seen himself returning for more than a weekend. There were too many ghosts haunting him here. Too much potential for uncomfortable conversations and drama—Grey hated both.

"Absolutely. Moonlight Ridge is in dire straits financially so we have to open the brewery as soon as possible. There isn't nearly enough revenue to sustain operations."

"I'm aware." Grey's knack for numbers had prompted Mack to ask him to look at some of the inn's financials after Jameson came home from the hospital. There were irregularities to say the least. Grey suspected someone had their hand in the cookie jar, but it would take a trained eye to find the culprit and learn how they were stealing. "I've hired the forensic accountant. Since so much of the business's records are on paper, I asked her to come and stay. I booked her in one of the guest cottages."

Mack peeked under the lid of the file box on the desk, then closed it, shaking his head in dismay. "That's a relief. I have no idea where we would even start."

"Since Pops is living down on the first floor while he recovers, we should be able to sneak up here and remove these extra files pretty easily."

"We definitely don't want him to know about this. He can't be under any stress," Mack said. "We should probably keep it a secret from Giada, too. I don't know how much she tells him."

"Where are those two, anyway?"

"Out for a walk with the dogs. You should see them together. It's hilarious. She gripes at him, he grumbles back, and then they end up laughing. I think love might be in the air."

Grey moved a stack of papers from the end of the leather tufted sofa and took a seat. "Love?" Grey didn't want to sound so incredulous, but their Pops was recovering. Romance was messy. It should be the last thing on his mind.

Mack shrugged. "Molly and I picked up on it."

Mack had not only rekindled his romance with his childhood sweetheart since his return, they were talking about building a house on the resort grounds. Mack, the man constantly on the move, had decided to stay in Asheville. Permanently. "How is Molly? Everything still good with you two?"

Mack looked out the window and a goofy smile spread across his face. He had to be thinking about her. Was he *that* happy? It confounded Grey. He'd never felt that way about anyone. "Can you keep a secret?" Mack asked.

Grey nearly laughed. "I'm not known for gossip."

"I'm getting ready to propose to Molly. I got the ring. I want to set a date."

Grey couldn't fathom gathering so much enthusiasm for such a major life change, especially one that could end up being a mistake. But he also knew that once Mack decided to do something, it was going to happen, come hell or high water. "You must be nervous."

"Amazingly, I'm not. I already told her that I wanted to get married. And build a house together, and have a family. So this is just a formality, really. I guess I'm tired of sitting around and waiting for life to happen."

"You've hardly been sitting around. You're crazy successful. You've built an amazing business."

"It's not the same. I know that now."

Grey hoped his brother would still feel like that down the road. There were a lot of uncertainties at play. Still, he couldn't bring himself to express his own doubts. He and Mack were trying to rebuild their relationship. "Congratulations. I'm proud of you."

"Thanks. I'd like to get married here on the property."

"Makes perfect sense. It'll make Pops happy for sure."

"It could be good for Moonlight Ridge, too. Some positive publicity. The wedding business is falling off a bit, actually."

"I noticed when I took a look at the numbers." This was no small matter. The brothers had committed to bringing the family business back to its former glory *and* profitability. Weddings were a key component of that.

"Good. I was hoping you'd lend your critical eye to that aspect of the business. The same way you looked over the financials."

Grey's brain was ready to stomp on the brakes. "I know numbers and architecture. That's it. I know nothing about weddings."

"You don't need to. We just need someone to sort out how we turn around the financial side of it. We don't know if it's the source of the accounting irregularities, or if it's that we aren't keeping up with other venues because of being outdated. We're already addressing that with the renovations. But maybe it's not fast enough for the younger brides? Molly says the mothers tend to love Moonlight Ridge, but daughters want something modern. Then again the other possibility is that it's our wedding planner, Autumn Kincaid. She's gotten some negative press attention."

"For what?"

"Her dad is Leo Kincaid, so she ends up on gossip websites every now and then. Her fiancé canceled their wedding at the last minute, so they've been having a field day with it."

Grey didn't follow entertainment closely, but he would've had to have been living under a rock to not know about Leo Kincaid. The man had been accused of sexually harassing dozens of women in Hollywood over the course of his career. "Wow."

"I know. This is uncharted territory. We've never had a controversial employee like this. And we're losing business because of the drama. A lot of these well-off families don't want anything to do with the resort. We have to nip this in the bud."

"You could suspend her contract."

Mack shook his head. "I'm hoping you can save it before it comes to that. She's Molly's best friend. Dad really likes her. And we have several big weddings this summer that we need Autumn here for."

Grey was still unsure of his ability to help with any of this, but weddings were important to Moonlight Ridge, and part of coming to Asheville for the summer was to be a better son and brother. He had to try. "Something tells me she's not going to like my interfering. Especially since I know nothing about the topic."

"It's better that way. You can walk in with fresh eyes," Mack said.

From downstairs, there were voices and a few barks. Giada and their dad were back from their walk with the two golden retrievers.

"Grey? Are you here? I saw a strange car out front." Jameson's voice boomed even at a distance.

"That's my rental, Pops. Mack and I are on our way

down." Grey made for the door at the same time as his brother. "I feel like you're trusting me with a lot right now," he said to Mack.

Mack looked like he wanted to fling his arm over Grey's shoulder, but wasn't sure of Grey's reaction. Instead he said, "It's all hands on deck. We desperately need your help."

and with every step of her ascent, more of the cottage came into view. Clad in natural stone with a gray slate roof and tall paned windows, she already knew it took good advantage of the beautiful mountain views.

But then a different kind of view entered her field of vision, making her come to a halt. Grey Holloway was doing push-ups on his patio. She stood there for a moment, just watching as his arms flexed with every rep. His biceps rounded, the contours of his muscles drew tighter, and beads of sweat glistened on his skin. *Oh my.* Yes, it was June, but the air around her suddenly felt unseasonably hot. Downright sticky. When her family vacationed at Moonlight Ridge when Autumn was younger, Autumn spent the whole time with Molly. She'd only seen Grey from a distance before, and only for a fleeting moment the last time he'd been at Moonlight Ridge. She'd had no idea he was hiding such a chiseled physique under his crisp dress shirts. Maybe working with Grey wouldn't be half-bad after all.

She wasn't quite sure how to interrupt his workout, but she also knew that it would be far worse for her if he were to stop, look up and see her standing in what was practically the bushes. Pondering her best approach, she cleared her throat. He just kept going. She tried a second time, louder, but he was laser-focused. Persistent. Up. Down. Up. Down. More glistening. Even more flexing. *How many push-ups can one guy do?* She decided she didn't have time to find out.

"Hello," she called, resuming her trip up the path. "Good morning. I'm sorry to interrupt you."

Grey straightened his arms at the top of a rep and

turned his head, glaring at her. It was her first glimpse of grumpy Grey. He scowled at her. *Scowled.*

Autumn second-guessed her decision to try this approach, but there was no turning back now. She was here and she had muffins. She'd just have to turn around Grey's sour state. "I'm sorry for showing up unannounced, but I didn't know the best way to reach you, so I thought I'd stop by."

She reached the end of the path and the edge of the patio just as he popped back up to standing. He was... *wow.* Stunning was the first word that popped into her head as he grabbed a towel and wiped the perspiration from his face. He was tall and extremely fit with sculpted shoulders and a trim waist. His thick brown hair was shorter on the sides, pleasingly tousled on top and a bit damp with sweat, as was his T-shirt, which clung to his defined chest in all the right places. Even from where she stood, she could see how intense his blue eyes were—dark and stormy.

Or perhaps that was shock.

"Really. I'm sorry," she blurted. "I should've found a way to let you know I was coming by." *Why do you do this? Think, Autumn. Think.*

"You're Autumn Kincaid." His voice was deep and even, showing no emotion, which was actually a good sign. At least his tone didn't suggest that he was downright angry. Still, there was very little that was welcoming in either his stance or his demeanor.

"That's me. I understand we're going to be working together." She lifted up the bakery box she was carrying in one hand. "I brought breakfast."

He narrowed his sights on the package. "I don't usually eat before lunch."

Now *that* she had not planned on. No wonder he looked like solid muscle. "Maybe today's the day you mix up your routine. I make a habit of doing new things as often as possible. It makes life much more interesting."

He stared back at her, seeming utterly confused. "Life is plenty interesting without trying to make it more so." He shook his head as if he was trying to rattle loose a few thoughts. It definitely made her curious about what might be going through his mind right now and how that might relate to her. Hopefully he didn't think she had a screw loose, but if he did...well, he wouldn't be the first.

She took the initiative and set her breakfast offerings down on the wood outdoor dining table where he had a water bottle sitting. With a cleansing breath, she offered her hand. "Let's start over. I'm Autumn Kincaid. I specialize in wedding planning, delivering unwanted breakfasts and interrupting people while they're exercising."

A slight smile curved one corner of his mouth, which she not only took as encouragement, she found quite enticing. It certainly made her want to try to get him to do it as often as possible. He wiped his hands with the towel before hesitantly returning the handshake. "Grey Holloway. I specialize in push-ups and awkward greetings, apparently. I'm sorry, but you surprised me."

This might not have been Autumn's best idea, but

she couldn't exactly go back in time and try again. "Next time, I'll call. Remind me to get your number."

He smiled again, the expression in his eyes softening. "Will do." He looked down at the table. "Please. Have a seat."

"Thank you." Autumn pulled out a patio chair and got situated. "Will you at least have some coffee?"

"Always." Grey sat right next to her. "I apologize for my choice of attire. If I'd known we were going to have a business meeting, I would've dressed for it."

Autumn glanced at him again, trying to figure him out. She'd spent only short stretches of time around Mack, Grey's brother, and she knew that all three brothers were adopted, but it was still surprising to see how different they were from each other. She handed Grey one of the cups she'd brought, along with a few creamers and packets of sugar. "I wasn't sure how you take your coffee."

He took a sip. "Black is good. Thank you."

Autumn shuddered at the thought. She ripped open three sugar packets, removed the lid from her cup and dumped them in. "I don't know how you can drink it that way."

He shrugged. "This is how I always have it."

"I need it at least a little sweet. Takes the edge off the bitterness."

Again, he regarded her with those questioning eyes of his. It was as if she was a puzzle he was trying to solve. If only he knew she was doing the same thing— sorting out whether he was going to stick a pin in the only thing she had going for her—planning weddings at Moonlight Ridge.

He took another sip of coffee. "I don't really like the bitterness either. I think I'm just used to it."

Grey didn't quite know what to make of Autumn, but he was certain of one thing—she was gorgeous. Her wavy dark blond hair tumbled past her shoulders, a striking complement to the dark-framed glasses she wore, which made her look so studious. He was definitely drawn to that. Her personality, however, was a complete one-eighty from his own. Perhaps this was simply how wedding planners behaved, endlessly upbeat and sunny, but it didn't align with the situation he knew her to be in. Her job was on the line. And she was stuck with an architect meddling in her business.

"I have to say," he started. "You seem very happy for a woman who was recently the subject of national gossip about her fiancé leaving her."

Autumn's brown eyes went wide with shock. "Wow. You don't mess around. Just jumped right in to the ugliest part of the conversation, didn't you?"

"It's the truth, isn't it?"

"It is. Just like it's the truth that I had a mouth full of metal and terrible skin when I was fifteen. Maybe you'd like to see some photos of me as an awkward teenager?"

Now it was Grey's turn to be surprised. He hadn't meant to prompt such a heated response. "I'm sorry if that was too personal. I was only saying that you seem very happy. I'm not sure I would be if I was in your situation."

"If I let myself get dragged down into misery every time something bad happened, I'd never ever be happy. Luckily, I'm an optimist for the most part."

Although Grey would never describe his personal default as happy, he did appreciate the idea of accepting one's natural disposition rather than allowing circumstance to dictate it. That was the point he'd tried to prove by not eating what she'd brought from the bakery.

"Plus, I can't afford to be dour," she continued. "Couples want an upbeat wedding planner. They want someone who doesn't get fazed, and can handle any problem at any time while never dropping her smile."

"So it's an act?"

"If I need it to be."

This felt like another sliver of common ground with Autumn. Grey had learned long ago that obscuring the extremes of emotion steadied his life. When Grey was very young and still living with his biological parents, he did his best to be perfectly behaved, so as not to provoke either of them. His father had a very short fuse and his mother was an alcoholic, which ultimately proved a fatal combination. As for later in life, the one time Grey had truly let loose with his feelings, he and his brothers ended up at the bottom of a ravine. "I appreciate your commitment to your job. We need that professionalism at Moonlight Ridge."

A soft breeze blew Autumn's hair from her face. She had flawless peachy skin, full lips colored deep rose, and her inner sunniness radiated from within. He had to wonder what her fiancé had been thinking when he decided to leave her, especially with such inopportune timing. "It's more than being professional. I work with people at a time that's both happy and incredibly stressful. I fail if I don't take away their worries so they can focus on the good of it. Otherwise, I might ruin one of the most important days of their lives."

Grey could've easily launched into his opinions about marriage, and how that important day often ended up being nothing more than a sad reminder, but now seemed like a bad time. "I had no idea so much psychology went into planning weddings."

"Sometimes I feel like a therapist, but it's really just about listening and being empathetic." She smiled sweetly and opened up the bakery box. As she pulled the string and lifted the lid, the aroma of baked goods hit his nose much stronger. She pulled out a large muffin for herself, then slid the box across the table to him.

Grey held up his hand. "Oh, no thank you. Like I said, I don't normally eat breakfast."

"This isn't breakfast. It's a personality test. If you can resist what's in that box, I'll know that I've read you correctly."

"It's not a flaw in my personality if I don't eat a muffin."

"There are scones in there, too. And I'm not saying it's bad, but I want to know how stubborn you are."

"I'm not stubborn."

"He said stubbornly…"

Grey wanted to feel frustrated, but the truth was that he was enjoying the back-and-forth with Autumn, even when he was determined not to smile and show her. When his brothers and Jameson challenged him, it was far less fun. "I can resist anything. I have incredible willpower."

"You don't get tempted? Ever?" She peeled back the paper wrapper with her perfectly manicured fingertips and took a bite of the muffin. She closed her eyes as sheer bliss bloomed on her face. "Mmm. This is so good. Apple cinnamon. It's like a sugary hug." Her eyes slowly drifted open and she licked her lower lip.

Suddenly Grey was thinking too much about temptation and Autumn's mouth. It had been a long time since he'd been alone with a woman. Even though they were technically in a business meeting, the thought did cross his mind that he wouldn't mind taking off her glasses and digging his hand into her hair, curling his fingertips into her nape and kissing her. It was a purely carnal thought, with no emotion attached. Grey didn't believe in romance. But he did believe in sex. "I'll take your word for it."

"There's a passionfruit Danish in there, too. It's insanely good. Sweet and sticky. Absolutely delicious."

Grey felt tension growing in his hips, while the sugary aroma teased his nose and Autumn teased *him*. But he would not give in. He would not show the slightest weakness. It wasn't about the pastries. It was about demonstrating that he couldn't be swayed so easily. Not by sweets. Or beauty, for that matter. "I'm good. Thank you."

A frustrated tut left her lips. "Fine. Suit yourself."

Grey stifled a smile. He didn't want to gloat about sticking to his guns. "Did you want to talk about actual work this morning?"

"Yes. I would. Molly told me that you and your brothers are concerned about my management of the weddings business here at Moonlight Ridge. I want you to know that although we've had a few cancellations, it's only a minor hiccup and everything is on track. We're going to have a very busy fall and holiday season."

Grey took another sip of his coffee. "Okay. Well, I know this isn't a fun topic, but what about that bad bit of publicity? We have very exclusive clientele for weddings, don't we? Well-established, wealthy families? I doubt they want to risk working with someone who's attracted even the slightest bit of controversy. No one wants to end up in the headlines themselves."

"The tabloids don't care about our clients. They care about embarrassing me."

"Do you think it's because of your father?"

"It definitely is. Which is why I don't have any contact with him anymore, which is the main reason I moved to Asheville in the first place. To stay away from it. To stay away from him."

"It seems like the controversy has followed you anyway."

"The gossip rags will take any excuse to write about Hollywood royalty, cast down in disgrace. Also, these people think I was born with a silver spoon in my mouth."

Again, the thought of Autumn's mouth was distracting. Just the way it moved when she talked was enticing. It made him want to hear more. "And were you? Born with a silver spoon?"

"If you're asking if I grew up in a high-profile family, with everything I could have ever wanted, then yes. But my background makes me uniquely suited to do this job. I can relate to these powerful families. I understand the dysfunctional ways they work. I can tame the spoiled bridezilla. I've known dozens of women like that."

Grey's upbringing couldn't be any more different from Autumn's if he tried. Still, he could see her point. "You make a good case."

"This is why I don't think you and your brothers need to check up on me. I don't need help, Grey. Everything will be just fine. You can concentrate on the renovations, which will help me more in the long run. Every improvement is another reason to have a wedding here."

As he'd expected, Autumn didn't want him interfering. So why was he disappointed? Especially when he'd insisted to Mack that he wasn't qualified for this job? Was it Autumn? The bewildering blonde who was fun to argue with? Maybe. "Let's make a deal. Book one big-dollar wedding to replace the one that just canceled, and I'll tell my brothers we need to back off."

Autumn finished off her muffin, then sucked a bit of sugar from her thumb. Grey tried not to stare, but still it sent a zip of electricity along his spine. "Define big-dollar."

"What was the largest wedding you did last year?"

"The Fitch-Knight wedding. They spent nearly one hundred grand."

"Can you book another like that?"

Her eyes grew comically large. "Weddings like that

don't grow on trees. I have one lead that might fit the bill. It's a tall order, but I'll try. Do you think that'll be enough to convince your brothers to let me do my thing without your supervision?"

"I think that'll be enough to call off the dogs."

She nodded again, slowly, seeming deep in thought. "Okay. Well, one thing Molly mentioned is that you might be able to help me with some of the old-guard Asheville families. I'm from LA. I don't have any long-standing ties to this city. Plus, having one of Jameson's sons on hand might help to seal the deal."

"People do love my dad."

"Of course. And if anyone can sell someone on a wedding here, it should be you." She looked back over her shoulder, surveying the lovely rolling hills that led down to the lake and the surrounding property. "You probably know more about Moonlight Ridge than almost anyone. I'm guessing you love it here."

Grey felt a distinct squeezing in the vicinity of his heart. He had loved it here at one time, but it didn't feel like home anymore. Time and distance were likely to blame, and much of that was on him since it had been his choice to stay away. But it wasn't like Mack and Travis hadn't done the same. They'd all needed their space after the accident that changed everyone's lives. "I like it. Sure. But if you're wanting someone to get misty-eyed and sentimental about it, that's not me."

Autumn nodded and closed up the bakery box. "That part doesn't surprise me."

"You think you have me figured out after one conversation?"

Autumn narrowed her eyes, sizing him up, and making his whole body go tight in a very pleasing way. "You work out a lot. You don't eat sweets if you can help it. You put your career first, second and third. You can't wait to get back to New York, because although you like Asheville, you don't love it."

"I assure you, there's more to me than that."

"Well, I can't wait to find out." She got up from her chair. "Can you be at my office Wednesday morning? Ten o'clock? Delilah Barefoot is coming to look at the grounds and get the full dog and pony show. Her mom is flying in from Washington, DC. Rebecca Barefoot? Have you heard of her?"

"The US Senator?" Grey stood, too.

"That's the one." Autumn was already sauntering away. He was mesmerized by the sway of her hips—she looked just as good going as she had arriving. Damn, he was in for a whole lot of trouble.

"I was supposed to remind you to get my number."

"I know where to find you."

Grey grumbled. Like he needed another surprise. "Hold on. You forgot the bakery box."

She stopped and looked back at him over her shoulder, her eyes flashing in the sunlight. It was the most potent glance Grey had ever endured. "I didn't forget. I'm thinking you could probably use a lesson in giving in to temptation."

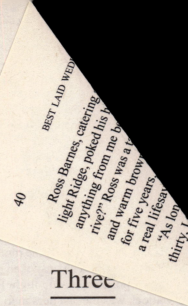

Ross Barnes, catering
light Ridge, poked his h
anything from me b
rive?" Ross was a t
and warm brow
for five years.
a real lifesa
"As lon
thirty, I
"I
shou
ci

# Three

Wednesday morning, the tiny third-floor office Autumn used to meet with Moonlight Ridge wedding clients was neat as a pin. This was not always the case. When she was up to her neck in planning, but wasn't expecting to meet with anyone in person, it tended to be organized chaos. Every available surface would be blanketed with seating charts and menus, reception playlists and books of linen samples. Not today.

Delilah Barefoot and her mother Rebecca, the US Senator, were coming to tour the Moonlight Ridge property, while Autumn would be working her hardest to convince them to book the wedding. Tap dancing. Begging. Groveling. Whatever it took. If she accomplished that, she'd have the big booking Grey said she needed to get his brothers off her back. She'd have breathing room.

...and events manager for Moon-
...ead into Autumn's office. "Need
...fore the bride and her mother ar-
...ll, lean man with close-cropped hair
... eyes. He'd been at Moonlight Ridge
... a few more than Autumn, and could be
...er.

...g as you're set to serve them lunch at twelve
...think we're good."

...elieve Chef has everything in order. I think today
...ld be okay." Ross stepped into the room. He'd exer-
...sed his usual diplomacy. The unspoken part was that
the executive chef position at Moonlight Ridge was in
flux. Fern Matlock was the last person to hold the job,
but she'd recently left for a "less stressful workplace."
Before her, it was French ex-pat Henri Bernard at the
helm, who left Moonlight Ridge to open his own restaurant. Now Hallie Gregson, Fern's sous-chef, was
in charge.

"How do you think it's going with Hallie?" Autumn
asked.

Ross shrugged. "As well as can be expected. She's
twenty-nine and doesn't have a lot of experience, but
Mr. Holloway seems committed to letting her grow
into the job."

Autumn sighed quietly. The food wasn't much of
a highlight at Moonlight Ridge, which made her job
more difficult. Still, she didn't begrudge Hallie her big
chance, especially since she knew Jameson had pro-
moted her after he discovered she was working two jobs
to make ends meet. "I'm sure she'll put it all together."

"Well, at least we have the wedding cake samples ready if your bride and her mother decide to test those today."

Autumn had a good feeling about Delilah. "I'm thinking that will be a yes. The bride's mother is flying in from Washington, DC. I can't imagine she'd take time from her busy schedule if they weren't fairly certain this was where they want to have the wedding."

"Well, you know I'm rooting for you. Always." Ross smiled warmly. He was truly one of the best parts of working at Moonlight Ridge. "Is it true that Grey Holloway is joining you for your meeting today?"

Autumn nodded, trying to keep from letting the idea of Grey make her nervous. Although she felt like she could handle him, he still held her fate in his hands. Plus, he was distractingly handsome, although she tried to think of that as a good thing. Maybe he could mesmerize the bride and her mom with his brooding eyes, strong jaw and perfect five-o'clock shadow. "Yes. The brothers want to be a bit more hands-on with weddings. It's such a big part of the financial health of the property. They need to know it'll be rock solid before they all return to the lives they had before Jameson got sick."

"Except for Mack. He's staying, right?" Ross wandered over to the window in her office. Although it could be drafty in the winter, it was on the front of the building and had a very pretty view of much of the property.

"Yep. Mack has officially said he's staying. It's Grey and Travis who will only be here temporarily."

"I don't see why the brothers have to get involved

in weddings at all. You and I run this part of the business like a machine. I worry about too many cooks in the kitchen." Ross adopted a pained expression on his face. Autumn chalked it up to his protective nature. "I mostly don't want them interfering with you and everything you've worked so hard for."

"It's fine. I can handle Grey Holloway." If only she felt as confident as her words suggested.

Ross looked out the window, then seemed to fix his sights on something. "Want a little gossip?" He turned to Autumn and arched one eyebrow.

"Is it about me? If so, I'll pass."

"No. Look." Ross waved her over and pointed outside.

All Autumn could see was a handful of people walking on the path that wound around the lake, and one of the landscapers tending a section of lawn. "What?"

"See that woman? With the long brown hair back in a ponytail?"

Autumn squinted. She'd opted for her contacts today, and she simply couldn't see as well when she wore them. "I guess? Who is she?"

"Grey Holloway's mysterious guest. Nobody knows who she is. You can't tell from this far away, but she's drop-dead gorgeous. A real beauty."

Autumn folded her arms across her chest. This was an annoying development, even when she had zero interest in romance and she and Grey were working together. She did like secretly admiring him, and it was just going to feel wrong if he was attached. So much for that little sliver of fun in her day. Of course, Autumn knew nothing about Grey's personal life, and he was incredibly smart, rich and easy on the eyes. It should come as exactly no surprise that he might have a girl-friend. "What do you mean nobody knows who she is?"

"She's staying in one of the guest cottages, but there's no name on the reservation. It simply has a month blocked out. I saw Grey personally bring up her bags. She's definitely staying a while. She had four huge suitcases."

That seemed odd, and not just because Moonlight Ridge had plenty of porters available to handle a job like that. "If she's his girlfriend, why wouldn't she be staying in his cottage?"

Ross shrugged. "Do you honestly think I've fig-ured out why the Holloways do anything? Jameson lets those three do whatever they want. Mack has practically taken over the place, and now we get Grey. It won't be long before Travis is here."

"They're his sons. And they're trying to make sure their dad is taken care of."

Ross bunched up his lips. "I still don't like it. Things were running just fine before they arrived."

"It won't be forever. Molly said Grey's only here for the summer, and Travis will be here through the fall and the first part of winter. We can get through that. No problem."

"It's June. December is a long way away." Ross looked at his smart watch. "I gotta run. Chef needs me. Just text me if you run into any rough spots today. And good luck." He walked out of her office.

Grey appeared in her doorway mere seconds

later, looking off down the hall. "Is that the catering manager?"

"Catering and events. Ross Barnes. Good morning to you, too."

Grey turned his attention to Autumn. In a dark blue dress shirt that made his eyes even more intense, and black trousers that accentuated his long, lean lines in ways a pair of gym shorts could not, he made her want to bite down on her lower lip. Or at the very least, a pencil. "Sorry. Good morning."

She waved him into her office. "Everything okay? You seem preoccupied."

"No. I'm fine."

Autumn wasn't sure if she should mention what Ross had clued her in on. It was none of her business. Then again, knowing the circumstances of Grey's personal life could help her. He held her future in his hands, after all. "I heard you have a friend staying on property." She decided that qualified as fact-finding and not gossip.

The most unpleasant look crossed his face. "Heard from whom?"

Autumn felt bad about even mentioning it. "Don't worry. Just someone on the staff."

He blew out a breath, but didn't take a seat. His posture was so stiff it made her uncomfortable just to see him that way. This was going to be a long day. "She's not a friend. She's a work associate."

That seemed like a peculiar answer. "Someone from your architecture firm? Are they helping with the design of Mack's brewery?"

Another frustrated grumble left his throat. "Not exactly. But close enough."

*Okay, then.* Autumn could take a hint Grey wasn't going to share and she'd pried enough. "Our bride and her mom should be here in about a half hour. Have a seat and I'll brief you on our potential clients and what we'll be doing with them today."

"I'm just observing, aren't I?"

He was acting as though he'd just arrived for a root canal, but she didn't like this any more than he did. "No. We need to work together. Our wedding customers spend tens of thousands of dollars. You're not following me around like I'm a trainee. It will look bad."

Everything in Grey's expression said that he did not get put on notice very often. Well, that was too bad. Autumn wasn't about to let him sink her ship. Her entire future was staying in Asheville and planning weddings.

"Okay, then. Show me the ropes."

Grey listened as Autumn explained who was coming in today. The upshot was this: important family, lots of money, this could be her one big booking. Grey would've taken all of those things as a positive a few days ago when Mack first asked him to oversee the wedding side of the business, but Autumn was wearing a royal blue dress that made her brown eyes sparkle. It made it incredibly difficult to concentrate.

"I noticed you aren't wearing your glasses today," he said, instantly regretting his decision to say anything at all.

"I try not to wear them when I meet potential clients.

I feel a little more polished without glasses. The trouble is I don't see as well with the contacts."

He was about to counter that he liked her in glasses. A lot. They were sexy. Not that Autumn was unsexy without them. Quite the contrary. She could make anything look alluring. But he decided it was best to keep his thoughts to himself. She'd only get the wrong idea. "I see."

"Anyway, Delilah is our bride. Her fiancé is Archer Morgan," Autumn said. "He works in banking down in Charlotte."

"I was on the swim team with an Archer Morgan in high school. He was two years younger than me."

Autumn smiled from ear to ear, her entire face lit up, and she clapped her hands together. "Grey! That's so perfect. You might actually end up helping me today."

Grey felt her excitement from five feet away. For a man who didn't get riled up, it was still infectious. He hoped he wouldn't ultimately end up disappointing her. "Maybe it's not the same guy."

"It has to be. How many Archers do you know?"

"Just one."

"Well, this is my first. I'm sure it's him. I will definitely need you to play up your connection. Make sure the bride knows he's your buddy."

Grey wasn't a "buddy" sort of guy. "We weren't friends. We were teammates."

"Just tell her that you liked him. That you remember him." She flipped through her three-ring binder. "This would be a big wedding. They're thinking 300 guests. In my experience, when people with lots of money and power have a wedding, the guest list is always bigger than they first estimate. So this would max out our capacity. The most we've ever done is 380."

"Sounds promising."

"Also a logistical nightmare."

"What's another eighty people? More chairs, more food. That doesn't seem like a big deal."

Autumn dropped her chin and he really missed the glasses as she delivered a look that was both admonishing and seriously hot. The thought of those dark tortoiseshell frames on the tip of her nose did something to him. He loved how strong she was. So comfortable in her own skin. "It's huge. We won't have nearly enough parking, which means shuttle buses and drivers. We'll have to block out a large number of rooms and cottages, so we have to hope there aren't any existing reservations that need to be moved around. Then there are extra bathrooms and staff and a million other things I haven't even mentioned."

"And you do all of this on your own?"

"Yes. I'm a one-woman show."

It occurred to Grey that Autumn's position at Moonlight Ridge might be more complicated than he and his brothers had first thought. "I had no idea."

Autumn pointed at him with her pen. "That's why I'm showing you the ropes." Her phone buzzed with a text. "Looks like they're here. We'd better head down to the lobby." She rose from her desk, breezed past him to a storage armoire, then opened it to reveal a full-length mirror. "How do I look?"

He got up out of his chair, watching as she scrutinized herself, cocking her head to one side and swiveling her hips enough to make the hemline of her dress swish. He hadn't fully appreciated just how lovely her legs were. Apparently, he'd spent too much time admiring the rest of her. *Amazing. Gorgeous.* He suddenly found it hard to swallow. "Fine."

She looked back at him over her shoulder, just like she had out on the patio of his cottage. Her gaze was so powerful. It was like lightning in a bottle, even when it was clear she was disappointed. "That's all you're going to say?"

"I didn't want to lay it on too thick."

She closed the cabinet door and stepped closer, placing her hand on his shoulder. Her touch sent warmth rippling through him. "It's not possible to lay it on too thick when a woman asks how she looks."

"It's still not my thing."

"At the very least, I'm going to need you to muster some enthusiasm for something. Otherwise, this booking is not going to happen." With a turn on her heel, Autumn marched out into the hallway.

Grey waited for a moment, trying to compute what she'd said. It wasn't his job to make this happen. It was hers. Still, he'd promised his brothers he'd help and he wasn't about to let them down. He hustled to catch up with her, and trailed behind her down two lengthy flights of stairs to the ground floor. He did his best to ignore the sexy sway of her hips, and the sweet fragrance left behind from every swing of her long blond hair.

When they arrived downstairs in the lobby, it was immediately apparent who they would be meeting with. Rebecca Barefoot was standing off in the corner, talking on the phone. Petite in stature, with perfectly coiffed short red hair and a face he recognized from the news, Rebecca had an air about her that took no time to identify. He'd had hundreds of powerful clients over the years. *This* he could handle.

"You must be Delilah." Autumn walked up to the younger of the two women and extended her hand.

"Yes. Hi." Delilah looked exactly like her mother, except her red tresses were long and wavy.

"Allow me to introduce Grey Holloway," Autumn said. "His family owns the resort. I also believe he knows your husband-to-be."

"Really? What a coincidence," Delilah said.

Grey shook her hand. "Yes. We were on swim team together in high school. He's a great guy. If you book your wedding here, I look forward to having the chance to catch up with him." He hoped that would suffice.

"And I'm sure Archer will be thrilled to know that an old friend is one of the owner's sons." She glanced over at her mother. "Sorry. She's on the phone. This will happen a lot. I'm used to it."

Rebecca tucked her phone into the sizable designer handbag hanging on her arm, then turned and introduced herself. "Rebecca Barefoot." She heartily shook hands with both Autumn and Grey. "I apologize. I've promised my daughter I'll keep the phone calls to a minimum today. I would like it if we could get started though. I have an incredibly tight schedule."

Autumn smiled, but Grey could tell that it was forced. She was in wedding planner mode. He made a vow to follow her lead. On everything. "Well then," Autumn said. "Let's begin the tour."

They started with the main inn, which was the historic original building on the estate, constructed circa 1930. Since then, many additions had been made, the largest of which was in the 1950s when two large wings were tacked on. The finishes—carpet, tile, woodwork and lighting had all been the finest available when they were installed. But since then, parts of the inn were showing their age. Grey and his brothers agreed they needed updates after Mack came home to help with Jameson's recovery and reported back on the inn's condition. They got things started right away, but renovations were a slow process, as they wanted to remain open while updates were made. With crews handling small blocks of rooms at a time, it was going to take months.

Autumn described the various amenities available to guests and explained the system for reserving room blocks. They next toured the main ballroom, which had reportedly been quite the location for parties in the 1930s. Now, it was where most indoor wedding receptions were held. All the while, Autumn did an expert job explaining everything, making the history of the property sound far more romantic than Grey had ever heard. As she warmed to Rebecca and Delilah, she became even more genuine. One thing he was sure of—

Autumn was amazing at her job. She belonged here, despite the problems she might have brought to their weddings business.

Next they walked outside and strolled down the winding paths leading behind the inn to the garden, which even Grey could admit was a lovely spot. Although it was carefully manicured—tidy hedges, rose bushes and perennials in full bloom, the meadow beyond it was an untamed sea of wildflowers, skirted by lush green forest.

"This *is* a beautiful spot." Rebecca took survey of the garden. There was no mistaking the "but" hanging in the air. She had reservations. It was just a matter of how Autumn would handle them.

"It's so pretty," Delilah said. "I really think it's perfect. It's so grand and steeped in history. It's like a fairy tale. I absolutely love it."

"I can tell," Rebecca said.

"I wasn't sure I would," Delilah replied. "I was worried it would be too old-fashioned. That's sort of the reputation of Moonlight Ridge, unfortunately."

Grey hated hearing the criticism, but he and his brothers knew that was the perception. It happened with any historic property—the age was part of the appeal but also a hindrance. "We're in the process of updating a great deal of the facilities." He wanted to let Autumn take the lead, but he had to chime in and defend the resort. "Including guest rooms. My brother owns Corkscrew Craft Beer Breweries and I'm helping him with the plans for a brewery right here on the grounds. It could be a great spot for a rehearsal dinner. We should also be breaking ground on our new state-of-the-art spa before the end of the summer. If you're looking at next June, it will be open in time for you and your bridal party to enjoy the facilities."

"That sounds amazing," Delilah said.

Rebecca slid her daughter a look. "Darling, you know that's not the main reservation I have. I promised you I'd come and look, but I'm not sure this is the right choice. Like it or not, my job is a consideration."

"My wedding is more than an opportunity for publicity, Mother. And it's ultimately my choice." Delilah turned her back on her mom, and walked closer to the center of the garden.

"If you don't mind me asking, what are your reservations, Ms. Barefoot?" Autumn asked.

Rebecca pursed her lips tightly. "I don't like the attention you've received in the media lately, Ms. Kincaid. When my PR person found out we were visiting here today, she begged me to cancel. There's just no reason to invite that kind of controversy when my daughter is getting married. It should be a happy day. Not a ding to my professional reputation."

All color drained from Autumn's face. "I assure you that I will do my best to remain in the background. And I no longer have any ties to my father."

"Have you issued a formal statement? Because I've supported laws meant to take down men like your father. I can't be associated with that."

*Ouch.* Grey had thick skin, but he couldn't help but

feel bad for Autumn, especially when she looked truly shell-shocked. Surely she'd never encountered venom like this while planning a wedding.

"A formal statement?" Autumn asked. "I'm a wedding planner, Ms. Barefoot. I don't really deal with things like that."

"And I'm a very powerful woman who can't afford to make a single mistake."

"Mom. Stop it," Delilah turned and begged.

Grey felt his blood at a simmer, listening to this woman be so uncommonly cruel to Autumn and not particularly nice to her daughter, either. He couldn't watch or listen to this any longer. "Ms. Barefoot, can you and I have a chat for a moment? Just the two of us?"

She looked startled by the request. It seemed as close to an upper hand as Grey was going to get. "For a minute."

Grey escorted Rebecca over to a quieter corner of the garden. "I understand where you're coming from. I own an architecture firm in New York and the power of appearances cannot be underestimated. But I would venture that Ms. Kincaid's reaction to your line of questions should tell you everything you need to know about her and her character."

Rebecca narrowed her eyes with suspicion. "I don't know that I see where you're going with this."

"You caught her completely off guard, and I've seen Autumn handle plenty of difficult situations without getting fazed." That wasn't entirely true, but he would take Autumn's word for it. "To my knowledge, she doesn't have any contact with her father. That's why she lives in Asheville. She left behind a life of privilege and glamour in Los Angeles, just so she could create distance between herself and him."

"I suppose there's something to be said for that."

"And as for her skills as a wedding planner, let me tell you that she will handle every detail perfectly without skipping a beat. Honestly, she'll take a lot of heat off you. You won't have to do anything other than show up. As a busy woman, you must be able to appreciate that."

"I do."

Grey pointed to Autumn and Delilah, who were animatedly talking. Delilah even laughed. "And see that? That's what you're getting when you have a wedding here. Every member of the staff will give your daughter personal attention, especially Autumn. She genuinely cares. We all do."

Rebecca eyed Grey up and down. "Is that why the owner's son, an accomplished architect no less, is tagging along to give a bride and her mom a tour?"

"What can I say? I care a lot." Grey knew then that despite his reservations about returning to Moonlight Ridge for the summer, he truly did care and it had been the right choice. He hoped he would feel that way when it was time to return home to New York.

"Okay, then. If this is what Delilah decides, I'm good with it." She delivered a penetrating stare. "But if there's a single problem, I'm going to get you to host a fundraiser here for me on your dime."

Grey forced himself to smile. "That sounds perfect."

Grey and Rebecca walked back over to Autumn and

Delilah. "Grey convinced me that everything will be okay. So if this is what you want, Delilah, I give it my stamp of approval."

"Really?" Autumn blurted, quickly choking back the question. "I mean, that's wonderful."

"Thank you, Mom. And thanks to you, too, Grey," Delilah said. "I want to bring Archer back to give it a tour, but this is what I want."

Autumn smiled wide. "Fantastic. If you want to head back into the inn, we can talk some more and I'll take you in to have lunch. I just need a minute with Grey."

Rebecca and Delilah trailed into the building. "What did you say to her?" Autumn asked. "You didn't just become Moonlight Ridge's new wedding planner, did you?"

"What? No. Of course not. I just told her that the staff at Moonlight Ridge would take care of her and her daughter. That she wouldn't have to do a thing. I said some nice things about you, too."

"That was enough for her to change her mind? Five minutes after she looked like she wanted to spit on me? That seems unlikely considering that you don't like to lay it on too thick."

"I thought you would be happy about this. We got the booking, didn't we?"

Autumn blew out a breath. "*You* got the booking. It's not going to help with getting you or your brothers off my back."

So that was what this was really about. Autumn wanted him out of her business. He was a nuisance to her. It was probably for the best. She was a distraction when he needed nothing of the sort. He didn't need one more thing to be immersed in at Moonlight Ridge. "Don't worry. I won't tell my brothers what happened. All the credit will be yours."

# Four

---

Friday morning, Grey was practically out the door for his meeting at the new brewery space when Mack called.

"Hey. Have you left yet?" Mack asked.

"Just about to."

"What's your morning like?"

"Why? Do you have to reschedule?" Grey didn't want to be irked, but he was. This was so typical for Mack. As the oldest, he had this knack for wanting Grey, and Travis for that matter, to bend to whatever he wanted.

"No. I'm over at Dad's house having coffee with Giada and him. Why don't you come by? I'll drive us out to the site right after."

Grey wasn't sure why this all seemed odd, but it

did. Probably because the barn destined to become the brewery and Jameson's house were on near-opposite ends of the Moonlight Ridge property and it wasn't like Mack to delay any discussion of his business. Efficiency and the bottom line always came first for Mack. Or at least they had before he returned to Asheville and fell madly in love.

"Okay. Fine. I'll be there in ten." Grey didn't see that he had a choice but to acquiesce. Plus, he did want to see his Pops. With his laptop bag slung over his shoulder, he made out on foot for the house, arriving pretty much exactly when he'd said he would. He knocked to announce his arrival, then let himself in. Laughter filtered into the foyer, and for a moment, Grey was once again feeling as though he was traveling between the present and the past.

Giada, Mack and Pops were smiling ear to ear when Grey walked into the kitchen, where the three were gathered at the large center island.

"Good morning, Grey," Giada said. "Let me get you a cup of coffee."

Mack beelined for Grey, giving him a slightly awkward hug. There was still uneasiness between them, and Grey was painfully aware of it. "Hey. Thanks for coming by."

Grey's first thought was that something was up. He looked Mack square in the eye. "Did I miss something? I feel like I did."

Mack sucked in a deep breath and grinned. "Molly and I are officially engaged. I gave her the ring last night."

Grey took a second to digest the announcement. "Wow. Congratulations. I'm so glad." He knew he was being reserved, but it wasn't in his nature to gush about anything, no matter how joyous it might seem. It didn't mean he was any less happy for his brother.

Giada, who was normally far more fiery than frivolous, nearly squealed as she handed Grey his cup of coffee. "It's so wonderful."

One look over at his dad and Grey knew exactly how thrilled he was with the news—he looked like he was going to burst open with glee. Grey had never seen him smile like that. "Pops. You must be over the moon." Grey stepped over to his dad, who was perched on a bar stool at the island, and gave him a hug.

"It's the best news since I landed in the hospital. I can tell you that much." Pops held Grey for a few extra seconds, but this was the norm. Everything the man did projected how much love he had for you.

"Did you set a date?" Grey took a sip of his coffee.

"And you're getting married on the property, of course," Pops said.

Mack nodded. "It only makes sense. As for the timing, we're hoping the end of summer. Maybe the weekend before Labor Day."

"Are we talking a big wedding? That might not be enough time to plan everything." Grey hardly knew what was coming out of his mouth. Not long ago, these questions wouldn't have even occurred to him. But that was before he met Autumn and became immersed in the business of weddings at Moonlight Ridge.

Mack laughed. "Listen to the aspiring wedding planner."

"Screw off!" Grey left it at that. Any detailed talk of business would just make Pops nosy. "What about Travis? I thought he wasn't coming back until early September."

"I'll just have to beg him to come back that weekend. I know he's busy, but we can't do it over Labor Day. The inn is fully booked," Mack said.

This was good news. Moonlight Ridge had been struggling with occupancy, too. Maybe the brothers were making a difference by implementing Molly's ideas.

"As for the size, we plan to keep it small. Maybe fifty guests. We just want to get married. No reason to make a big deal about it." Mack cleared his throat and cast Pops a sideways glance. "The venue is the only potential hiccup."

"How soon can you get the interior of the old barn presentable?" Pops asked.

It took Grey a minute to realize what they were thinking. And asking. "Where the brewery is going? By the end of August you want to have the ceremony in the barn?"

"We just want the building done. We don't need the brewery equipment installed. I know it's a lot to ask, but it's what we want. It'll be great publicity for the resort and the brewery. Plus, it's important to Molly and me," Mack said.

Grey ran his hand through his hair, his mind kicking into high gear with thoughts of everything that would have to happen. "Can our current contractor handle this?" They had two small crews on site, working on the guest room updates in the main inn. They were going to need a lot more manpower than that.

"Yes," Pops said. "I just got off the phone with Mountain Builders. They've got a large crew available and they're prepared to pull permits as soon as the design is complete."

"Your father called in some favors." Giada cast a disapproving look at Jameson. "Although I would prefer it if he didn't do things that get him so riled up."

"My son is getting married," Pops said. "I can't help it."

Grey took in a deep breath. There wasn't really a choice but for him to get on this runaway train. "The design is done, but I want Mack to see the renderings in the space before we move ahead." He pointed at Mack. "You and I need to get over to the site, ASAP, and talk through these plans."

"Got it." Mack took a final sip of his coffee, set down his cup, kissed Giada on the cheek and hugged Pops. "Thanks, you two. I'm excited."

Pops gripped Mack's arm and gazed up at him. "I'm proud of you, son. And happy."

Grey kissed his dad on the temple. "Bye, Pops. I'll see you later."

Mack and Grey strolled outside, both putting on their sunglasses, as the morning rays were intense. "Beautiful day," Mack said, heading for his car.

Grey couldn't think about the weather. He was too preoccupied with the timeline and everything that had to be done. Plus, Mack and Grey had more to discuss—Autumn and the forensic accountant. "I'm glad you drove. We need to save every minute we can." Grey climbed into Mack's black Mercedes, but as soon as he was inside, he had to fight off the flashbacks of the accident. He and Mack hadn't been in a car together in years and it was making too many memories come back. Fear. Chaos. The unholy sound of tires screeching, ending with a crash.

"You okay?" Mack revved the engine.

"Yeah. Let's get over there."

Ten minutes later, they arrived at the old barn, which was a remarkable building. The first floor was built entirely from local stone, with a second floor above made of timbers. It dated back to around the time of the original inn and would have been incredibly expensive to build at the time. Mack and Grey each grabbed a handle for one of the massive wood doors. The iron hinges squeaked in protest as they tugged them back. Sunlight flooded the relatively dark space, which was dirty, dusty and in need of a lot of attention. There were twenty-foot ceilings, an old hayloft and not much else. It had excellent bones though, and that was all Grey and Mack cared about.

Grey pulled his laptop out of his bag and rested it on his forearm, showing Mack the renderings of the final design. When the project was complete, there would be a stunning view of the lake from three sides of the building. They would situate the brewing operation along the back side of the building, which worked perfectly for access to the road for deliveries. Off to one side would be an open kitchen, serving up pub fare. A massive custom bar. A private dining room. A gift shop for brewery T-shirts. There would be gleaming floors fabricated from reclaimed lumber, and a mix of industrial and warmer furnishings like leather and wood to give a rustic, but upscale mountain vibe.

"Well? What do you think?" Grey asked.

Mack took several long strides ahead into the cavernous space, then turned around. "I work with some brilliant people, Grey, but I still can't believe what you see in this space. I knew it was doable, but I never imagined some of the ideas you came up with. It's perfect."

Grey was relieved. He'd really wanted to please and impress his brother. "Fantastic. I'll speak to the contractor so we can get this going. We have to run all of the plumbing and electrical before we can start on things like the floors. You're going to want the HVAC up and running by then, too."

"Nobody wants to be inside in August if there's no air-conditioning."

"Precisely."

Mack took another look around the space, seeming to understand what a monumental task they had ahead of them. "Do you think it can be done?"

However practical he liked to be, Grey didn't have it in his heart to disappoint his brother. "I do. I mean, I'll make it happen." In a lot of ways, he felt like he owed this to Mack. As to whenever he'd be able to make amends with Travis, he wasn't sure, but he hoped that could happen as well. The acrimony between them had gone on for too long.

"Thank you. I really appreciate that." Mack's phone buzzed with a text, which he glanced at quickly. "I have a conference call in a half hour with my master brewer. I should get going."

"I do need to talk to you about a few things."

"We can talk in the car."

They closed up the building and were soon on their way. "I wanted to let you know that the forensic accountant is making headway. Nothing definitive yet, but she's seeing some trends."

Mack glanced over at Grey. "And?"

"We'll know more soon."

"Okay. Sounds great."

"But you should know that some of the staff have talked about the fact that there's a mystery woman taking one of the cottages for a month. I worry that will send up red flags."

"Hopefully people will move on to other gossip. We don't want Pops finding out what she's looking for."

"Right. And then there's the matter of the wedding department." In a lot of ways, Grey felt like he was only getting started with understanding what Autumn did and whether that part of the business could be improved. But it was clear that Autumn did not want his help. "Autumn booked a very high-profile wedding for next summer. Senator Rebecca Barefoot's daughter. I really don't think we need to keep tabs on her anymore."

Mack shook his head. "I know that you're the one who sealed the deal, Grey. Autumn told Molly the whole story."

"What?" Why would she do that? Grey had perfectly

paved the way for her to get all the credit. All she had to do was take it.

"Autumn might seem like she's not a serious person at times, but trust me, she takes her job very seriously. She didn't want to take credit for something she didn't do."

Grey hadn't expected this at all. He'd let her off the hook, and she hadn't taken the opportunity to be rid of him. "You're telling me I need to continue to work with her? She doesn't want me around."

Mack pulled up in front of Grey's cottage, put the car in Park, then killed the engine. "Look. Part of the reason I asked you to step in with the wedding business was personal."

"Personal how?"

"Autumn is Molly's best friend and she worries about her. That means I worry about her. Being a wedding planner is the only thing she has and Moonlight Ridge is by far her biggest client. She's cut herself off from her family. Her fiancé dumped her. If she fails at this, it will be really hard for her to go start over somewhere else. Especially since Molly is almost like her sister."

Grey nodded, feeling the weight of family responsibility squarely on his shoulders. "I understand. You want Molly to be happy and she can't be like that unless her best friend is in a good place."

"Exactly. It's not just about keeping tabs on Autumn. It's about making sure she's successful. Not just for the business, but for her sake as well."

"I really hope you aren't holding me responsible for her happiness. That is not my area of expertise."

Mack laughed. "Believe me. I know you. Mr. Detached. Mr. Calm, Cool and Collected. Forget feelings."

"You make me sound like a robot."

"That's not how I mean it." There was a slight pause before he continued, "You know I love you."

That used to be so easy to say to each other growing up. Grey hoped one day things would feel natural again. "I love you, too. I'm glad we're working together. And I'm so happy you liked the plans."

"I'm happy about all of that, too. I hope Travis can come for the wedding. I'd love it if the three of us could spend some time together, especially now that Dad is doing better."

Grey nodded. "I'm sure we can work something out." He opened his door.

"So we're good with Autumn? You're going to continue to help her?"

Funny, but Grey didn't think of it as the task he had the first time his brother had asked. Not that he was going to share that with Mack. No way. There was zero reason to let on that he found himself enjoying his time with Autumn, even when she didn't seem to want him around. "Yeah. No problem."

Autumn was busy working at one of the tables in the Moonlight Ridge pub. Although she had both an off-site office and an office here on the third floor, Autumn liked working in the pub before it opened because it was quieter and she could spread out and use more table space. Plus, it had lovely light early in the day.

Out of the corner of her eye, Autumn spotted Molly sauntering into the room like she was floating on air.

"Good morning!" Molly practically sang her greeting, like a fairy tale princess.

"Good morning." Autumn noticed that her own voice sounded like a fairy tale ogre. She pushed aside a pile of spreadsheets. She couldn't stare at them any longer. It certainly wasn't improving her mood, which was admittedly a bit sour after the things Rebecca Barefoot had said the other day. She still couldn't believe she'd let that woman get to her. "What's got you so chipper?"

"Oh. I don't know. Just excited, I guess." Molly waggled the fingers of her left hand. The jumbo diamond-and-platinum ring was impossible to miss.

"Oh, my God!" Autumn jumped up out of her chair, unable to contain her excitement. "When did this happen? How did he ask?"

"Last night."

"Tell me everything."

"In typical Mack fashion, it wasn't a big elaborate thing. But it was still so romantic. We went for a walk around the pond at the back of the property, the one we used to swim in as kids, and we stopped to look at the moon. The next thing I knew, he was down on one knee with a box from the jeweler."

Autumn fought back the tears that threatened to sting her eyes. Some of what she was feeling was pure joy. Of course she was deeply excited for her best friend. But there was melancholy, too. She couldn't help but flash back to the night Jared had asked her to marry him. Autumn had been taken completely by surprise.

They'd only been dating for a few months, and although he had professed his love long before that, she hadn't been sure of the depths of his devotion. But he turned up one night at her house with a ring, a proposal and a suggestion that they move in together. He'd said he was determined to make a go of starting his own financial services company in Asheville. Autumn had thought that alone was a good sign. She figured that a man like him would only rearrange his life for true love. Little had she known that plan of his would never take flight. No, it wasn't true love. Even though Autumn had been convinced at the time that it was.

Autumn took Molly's hand in hers and admired the ring. "I don't think he needed to make it an elaborate proposal. I'd argue that this ring is doing all the talking."

Molly gazed down at it. "It's huge, isn't it?"

"It's beautiful. Absolutely gorgeous." The ring Jared had given to Autumn was not only a stunner, it was still sitting in a drawer in her kitchen. He hadn't asked for it back, and Autumn hadn't offered. It wasn't that she still had sentimental feelings about it. It was more about not being quite ready to admit defeat. She knew she had a hard time letting some things go. "So? Have you guys talked about a date? Please tell me you want to have it here and that you'll let me plan it."

"Of course."

A ribbon of delight wound its way through Autumn. She reached under the spreadsheets and pulled out her calendar. "What are you guys thinking?"

"The last weekend of August. Right before Labor Day."

Autumn blinked like crazy as she tried to compute this information. "As in ten weeks from now?" She looked up at Molly, hoping her expression could convey exactly how bonkers this was.

Molly gnawed on her thumbnail. "I know it's soon, but we really don't want a big wedding. Just something small."

"People say they want small and then it doesn't end up being like that."

"No. I'm serious. I'm thinking fifty people, tops. And Mack is talking to Grey this morning about starting the renovation for the barn. We'd like to get married there."

"You want to get married in a place that isn't actually suitable for a wedding, ten weeks from now."

"Yes. And I want you to be my maid of honor."

Any skepticism Autumn had was officially shoved to the back burner. It was not the maid of honor's job to be a downer. "Aww. That's so sweet. I'd love to. Thank you for asking me." Yes, this was all going to consume her summer. That was okay. It would keep her mind off Grey. If she tried really hard.

Molly shrugged. "I know it all sounds crazy, but it's what Mack and I want."

"Okay, then. We'll make it happen."

Molly leaned down and wrapped her arms around Autumn's shoulders. "Thank you so much. You're the absolute best."

Of course, Autumn knew that wasn't true. She'd

been striking out at work lately, particularly earlier that week. "I'm just happy for you."

"Thanks. I appreciate it." Molly took a seat across from Autumn. "Are you feeling any better about what happened with Rebecca Barefoot?"

"I'm okay. I'm just disappointed in myself. I froze up. She started talking about my family and I couldn't deal with it. I guess it's one thing to be on a gossip website and another when someone is right in your face."

"Of course. That makes perfect sense."

Autumn was happy about that, too. But now that she'd had some time to gather her thoughts about what had happened, she had this unsettled feeling in the pit of her stomach. She hadn't been kind or gracious about what he'd done, and it had been an act of chivalry. He'd done the right thing. And Autumn had let her ego get in the way of showing any appreciation at all. "Me too. Grey saved the day."

"Do you like working with him?"

"We hardly had a chance to get started before I messed up, so it's hard to say. But I like him. He's nice to have around, and he sure is nice to look at. " She stifled a sigh just thinking about exactly how much she enjoyed every chance she had to admire Grey. "He's also frustrating as hell. It's hard to know what he's thinking."

Molly nodded. "Mack says the same thing. All the time."

"That's not a good sign considering that they're brothers."

"Those three have their fair share of problems. That's

for sure." Molly glanced at the clock on the wall. "Oh, shoot. I'd better get to work. I have a million things to do." She made her way for the door, but stopped short and turned back to Autumn. "Oh. I forgot. Mack and I want to have a small engagement party on July Fourth. Before the fireworks. Put it on your calendar. He's hoping he can get Travis to visit."

"Do you need help with that, too?"

Molly held up her thumb and index finger with just a whisper of space between them. "A little bit. Not too much."

Autumn smiled as her best friend disappeared through the door. As soon as Molly was gone, Autumn's phone rang. It was Delilah Barefoot. "Hello? Delilah?"

"Autumn, hi. Do you have a minute? It looks like Archer isn't going to be able to tour the grounds with me right away, but I'd like to go ahead and firm up our date."

Autumn quickly grabbed her laptop, pulling up the shared catering and events calendar. "Of course. June 28th, right? A little more than a year from now. I wasn't about to let anyone take it without calling you first."

"Yes. We'd like to go ahead and sign the contract."

It was silly, but simply typing in "Barefoot-Morgan Wedding" felt like a step in the right direction. Autumn was playing her role. She'd felt left out and left behind the other day, but it had been her own doing. This was her chance to remedy that. "Fantastic. I will send the paperwork right away. We can schedule Archer's visit whenever you like. And feel free to call me any time with questions or to discuss details."

"Thank you so much. I appreciate that. I wouldn't have blamed you at all if you didn't want to deal with our wedding. My mother can be brash. I'm really sorry about everything that happened the other day."

"No need to apologize. It's not your fault. And everything she said was perfectly valid. My dad is not a good person, and I can understand anyone not wanting to be associated with him, even if it's only because I'm his daughter."

"But you can't help who your parents are. I feel the same way about my mom, and she's not nearly as controversial as your dad. You'd be surprised by the things people will say to me. They'll just walk up to me in a restaurant and tell me I'm despicable or that they feel sorry for me because they think my mom is a bad person."

Autumn hadn't realized until right then that she'd never met anyone who was in even a vaguely similar predicament to her own. She had friends back in LA with famous parents, but their moms and dads were beloved figures, not people with a name uttered in hushed tones with an edge of disgust. "I'm so sorry you've had to deal with that. But if it makes you feel any better, I completely understand how you feel."

"Thank you so much. I'm glad Grey turned things around with my mom. I guess he really sang your praises."

This came as a surprise. Autumn had assumed that whatever Grey said to Rebecca had been about selling Moonlight Ridge. It hadn't occurred to her that she might be her own selling point. "That's nice to hear. Thank you."

Delilah and Autumn said their goodbyes and Autumn rushed upstairs to her chaotic office. She quickly plugged Delilah and Archer's information into the standard Moonlight Ridge wedding contract and hit "print" on her computer. As the papers chugged their way out, Autumn glanced out the window overlooking the property. She owed Grey an apology. Or at least another thank-you. But she still hadn't taken his phone number. Sure, she could ask Molly for it. But something told Autumn that an in-person visit would be better.

Autumn collected the contract, sealed it up in an envelope, and gave it to Harry at the front desk to send by courier. Then she grabbed her sunglasses and hopped into one of the resort's golf carts and headed for Grey's cottage. When she arrived, she was a bit disappointed to discover that Grey was not out on his patio doing push-ups. She could only be so lucky. And today, she already felt lucky.

She went to one of the glass patio doors and rapped lightly on the frame. A few seconds later, Grey answered, looking just as confounded as he had when she'd shown up with baked goods. She couldn't deny just how good he looked in a decidedly more polished ensemble—dark jeans with a perfect fit and a white shirt with the sleeves rolled up to the elbows. She had a thing for forearms and Grey's were magnificent and strong, made all the more enticing by a chunky silver Breitling watch with a midnight-blue face on his wrist.

"We've got to stop meeting like this." Autumn hoped she sounded clever, not like a stalker.

Grey's expression immediately softened. "Right now. You and I are exchanging cell numbers."

"Don't you enjoy my little visits?"

"Yes. And no. I also think there's something to be said for using all available technology." He pulled his phone out of his pocket and Autumn fished hers out of her bag so they could finally take care of this small task. "Now that that's out of the way, what can I help you with?" he asked.

"I wanted to say I'm sorry for the way I acted the other day. You saved my butt and I should've been far more gracious about it."

"No need to apologize. I think anyone would've done what I did."

"Would they though? I get that you care about your family's business, but Delilah said you sang my praises to her mom. I wasn't aware we'd known each other long enough to get to the praise-singing phase of our relationship."

Grey laughed, a sound that made her think she was really breaking down walls between them. It was one of the sexiest sounds Autumn had ever heard. "Do you want to come in?"

Autumn shouldn't be feeling so delighted by the invitation, but she was. "I'd love to." She followed him inside, and they entered the great room on the back of the house, with wood-beamed cathedral ceilings, a large stone fireplace, a modern kitchen to one side, and truly breathtaking views down to the lake. "This is beautiful, Grey. Why don't all of the guesthouses look like this?"

Grey nodded. "Excellent question. That's one of those things my brothers and I are working on."

Autumn turned around in the cozy, but elegant space. She'd thought of Grey as the sort of guy who could only be truly comfortable in New York, with a bachelor pad decorated entirely in black and gray, but he seemed perfectly at home in a setting with a few softer edges. "I'm sure occupancy will go up after you do. Who wouldn't want to stay somewhere like this?" Through an open door, Autumn caught a glimpse of the bedroom—there was a big bed, dressed in crisp white bedding with a masculine brown tufted leather headboard. That seemed to work with Grey's personality, too. "So? Mack and Molly, huh? Pretty big news."

Grey stuffed his hands into the pockets of his jeans. "Yep. Hard to believe it, but one of the Holloway brothers actually fell in love."

Autumn perched herself on the arm of a leather club chair. "Is that really a surprise? It seems like a forgone conclusion. All three of you are ridiculously handsome and successful. Honestly, I'm wondering what Jameson was putting in your cereal bowls every morning when you were kids."

Grey arched his eyebrows. "Ah. But I don't eat breakfast."

"Oh, right."

"But seriously, no, it wasn't a forgone conclusion at all. We're all hyperfocused on our careers. Making time for things like romance doesn't always pay dividends."

"It's not a stock purchase."

"It's just a fancy way of saying it's not worth it."

"It *can* be worth it. If you meet the right person."

Grey shrugged. "I'm not the guy to ask. I don't believe in all of that."

Autumn got up from her seat and stepped closer to him. The instant she got a real whiff of his heavenly smell, she had to make a conscious decision to stop her approach before she was standing toe-to-toe with him. The urge to nestle her face in his neck and breathe in the warm and woodsy scent was a little too powerful. The thought of his facial scruff on her nose only added to the enticement. "All of what?"

"Love. It's something we construct in our minds. Or at least romantic love. The idea of staying with someone forever. I don't think we're meant to do that."

Autumn snorted in not-so-elegant fashion, but she could *not* believe the utter nonsense coming out of Grey's mouth. "You realize you're saying this to a wedding planner, right? My entire career is built on the idea that people are meant to do exactly that. Fall in love. Depend on each other. Take care of each other. Forever."

"Believing in that and your career choice don't have to be dependent on each other. Do your parents have a good marriage?"

"No. It was toxic. They're divorced now. But neither of them were faithful. I'm not sure they were ever really in love. I think they were caught up in the excitement of it. My dad's career was on the rise and my mom worked for him." Autumn didn't care to talk about her parents any more. It brought up too many memories of big fights and outrageous drama, like the night her mom broke every single dish in their kitchen in a fit of frustration over another of her dad's affairs, and ended up in an ambulance because her feet were all cut up. "That doesn't mean I don't believe in love and commitment. My grandparents had an amazing marriage."

"What happened to them?"

"They're still together. They're still in love. They're retired and they travel all the time, but I see them once or twice a year. They're really the only family I still see."

"Well, my parents were a horrible match, too. And I've never felt any need to permanently attach myself to anyone. Ever. And I can't imagine it, either, to be honest."

That struck Autumn as incredibly sad. Despite everything she'd been through, she still saw herself falling in love. She dared to see a long-term partnership with someone. Someday. "You never know when the right person will come along."

"And in the meantime, you spend a lot of time with the wrong people. You should know that better than anyone. How many months were you with your fiancé before things fell apart?"

Good God, Grey had a way of saying things that cut to the bone. "I don't care about that. It's the past. I'm looking ahead."

"But it just happened."

"More than three months ago. Ancient history as far as I'm concerned."

Grey pressed his lips together, seeming thoroughly unconvinced. "I think you're in denial."

"And I think we should talk about something else."

"Like what?" It wasn't really a question. It felt more like a challenge.

"How about the future of our working relationship?"

Grey took a step closer to her. "Why in the world did you tell Molly that you weren't the one who got the booking for the Barefoot wedding? That was your out."

Half of Autumn's brain was listening to his words. The other half was fixated on his shoulders—she'd seen them in a dress shirt, and she'd seen them doing push-ups, but she couldn't help but wonder what it would be like to touch them. To roll her fingers over what was surely a solid block of muscle. "It was the truth. I wasn't going to take credit for something I didn't do."

"You just put yourself in a worse position though. If you're fighting for your existence at Moonlight Ridge, you aren't making much of a case."

Autumn's frustration with Grey was only growing, partly because he seemed truly mad that she'd done something that would only mean they would continue working together. "I don't see it that way. I know that I'm good at my job. I make people happy and I find it very rewarding to do that."

Grey cast her another doubtful look. It was like he had a daily quota of doubt. "How do you see the bright side in everything?"

"I don't have a choice, Grey. Any other way and I wouldn't be able to function." She made her way to the door. "I'll get out of your hair now. I just wanted to stop by and say thanks again."

"Autumn, wait." Grey reached for her arm, and Autumn couldn't help but notice the zap of electricity between them when his fingers touched her elbow. Why was she so susceptible to Grey's charms? She didn't understand why he had any power over her at all. The man didn't believe in love. Aside from the fact that he was ridiculously sexy and incredibly smart, he was completely wrong for her.

"Yes?" she asked.

"When will we be working together again?"

"There's a wedding next weekend." Autumn scoured her brain for some reason she could see Grey before then, but then she scolded herself for being so attracted to him. "You can help me with that. See what my job is really like."

Grey smiled slightly, just enough to give her some encouragement. "I don't know that I'm dying to go to a wedding, but I do want to see you be successful. And you promised me you were going to show me the ropes."

"I absolutely did. And I always keep my promises." Autumn opened the door and stepped out onto the patio, but Grey followed her.

"I still don't understand why you outed yourself to Molly. I'm not entirely convinced it's because you couldn't stand to be anything less than honest. I have to think your survival instincts are stronger than that."

Autumn wasn't sure why she'd done it, either. It wasn't like Molly had tried to pry the information out of her. Autumn had given herself up. Maybe it was just that she wasn't eager to claim credit when it wasn't hers to take. Or maybe it was something else. "I don't know, Grey. Maybe I just like having you around."

# Five

Grey had been nothing less than completely honest when he'd told Autumn that he wasn't a big fan of weddings. He didn't really see the point. So much money and hoopla, knowing that 50 percent of marriages ended in despair and divorce. What person would walk into a casino and put down a year's salary, knowing they only had a one-in-two chance of winning it back? It was a risk only a fool would take.

Of course, Grey had his reasons for thinking this way. His parents' marriage had been dismal, never suggesting even the slightest glimmer of love or true affection. And when Grey was rescued from that situation, it was by Jameson, a single man who never seemed to want for a wife or commitment involving a ring, vows or a ceremony. It left Grey with only one conclusion—

romantic love was a trap. It was an illusion, a way to turn lust into something more meaningful or turn loneliness into something less persistent.

Still, he'd found himself oddly looking forward to this evening's Carter-Jackson wedding. He could admit that Autumn intrigued him, especially after making that comment the other day about liking having him around. When was the last time someone had actually said that about him? He wasn't sure of the answer.

Considering how many assumptions he'd made about Autumn, she'd turned out to be nothing like what he'd expected. She came from a famous Hollywood family, but seemed so immensely grounded, even when she had her head in the clouds. She'd allowed her fate at Moonlight Ridge to remain on the line, all because she couldn't bring herself to be anything less than painfully frank about what had happened when Rebecca Barefoot decided to be terrible about Autumn's past.

Wearing a charcoal suit, Grey strolled into the main ballroom, where the reception would be taking place. The actual ceremony was set to start in an hour, out in the garden behind the inn. The ballroom was abuzz with activity as members of the catering team set out water glasses and place settings on the dozens of round tables covered with white tablecloths surrounding the dance floor. At one end, the DJ was setting up lighting. Autumn, however, was nowhere to be found. He headed back out through the door and ran right into her.

Literally. She kicked his foot with one of her pointy-toed heels. Her head collided with his jaw.

"Oh my gosh. Grey. What the heck?" She jumped back, breathless, squinting, and rubbing her temple.

He couldn't ignore the way her voluptuous chest was heaving. In fact, he'd forgotten what his name was. Of course, that might've been the pain. His cheek was throbbing. "For all of that hair, you sure have a hard head."

"I could say the same thing for you. Good thing I'm wearing my contacts. You could've broken my glasses and then we would've been in serious trouble. I'm blind without them. Where were you going so fast?"

"I was looking for you." He reached for her shoulder to show his concern, but quickly learned that one touch would not be enough. He wanted to drag his fingers down the soft skin of her arm. "Are you okay?"

"I'm fine. Thank you." Autumn straightened and that was when he noticed her dress—a slim-fitting silhouette of sheer black lace with a cream-colored fabric underneath. It wasn't short. In fact, it fell below her knees. It wasn't low-cut. It was quite a modest neckline. But holy smokes did it show off every last delicious curve of the full hips that bloomed from her waist. "Are you okay? I should've worn my glasses tonight. That was stupid. It's probably my fault."

"It was an accident. I'm just glad that you're okay." Grey focused his attention on her face, if only to keep his eyes from roaming all over her luscious body. But that wasn't much help. Her lips were slightly parted, full and beckoning. Her eyes wide and intense. "Everything in the ballroom looks great," he said, trying to distract himself.

"Thank you. That's not the part I'm worried about. I'm looking for the groom. I got a text from his dad. He said his son is freaking out and wants to call off the ceremony. He's disappeared and this building is so huge, he could be anywhere."

"Oh." Grey hated drama, and this sounded like a whole heap of that.

Autumn looked at Grey, cocking her head to one side, and he could see the gears turning behind her beguiling brown eyes. "Come on. Help me look." She tugged on Grey's hand, then marched off down the hall. He had no choice but to go with her. "If we find him and he won't listen to me, maybe he'll listen to you."

"That's not a good idea. I can't convince someone to get married. Do you not remember the conversation we had the other day?"

Autumn shot him a look of pure annoyance. "I'm not asking you to persuade him to do anything. We just need to help him think straight. If the worst happens and we have to stick a pin in this wedding, there are horrible ways to do it and then there are slightly less horrible ways."

"Could that really happen? Does that really happen?"

"Not often, but yes. Love is messy, Grey." He and Autumn agreed on very little when it came to that topic—that was their common ground.

They jogged down one corridor, then another and another, doubling back at least once. But then they rounded a corner and sure enough, a man in a tux was standing at the very end of a narrow hall, staring out one of the many windows.

Autumn slowed her pace, approaching the groom with caution, like she was afraid she might spook him. "Max?" she called. "Can we talk for a minute?" Without looking back, she waved for Grey to come along.

The groom glanced over his shoulder then returned his attention to the world outside.

Grey still felt unsure of his role in this situation. He didn't deal well with people and feelings, especially when emotions were running high. "I really don't know what you expect me to do," he whispered.

"I'll do the talking. You can be the calming force," she muttered out of the side of her mouth.

*Calming force?* "You are the queen of armchair psychology, aren't you?"

"Call me whatever you want. Just do it later." A dozen or so strides and Autumn reached the man. She gently placed a hand on his back, which was the first time Grey noticed just how lovely her fingers were. "Max. How can I help?"

He didn't turn. In fact, he hung his head. "I'm overwhelmed. I'm trying to catch a breath and figure out what I'm thinking. And feeling."

Autumn moved closer and leaned against the wall, lowering her head in an attempt to make eye contact. "I get it. I totally get it. Today is a big day. It feels like so much."

Max turned to her. "Yes. Exactly. And I feel so embarrassed that I'm letting it get to me like this. I'm supposed to be strong. And I feel like I'm about to melt into a puddle."

Grey couldn't help it. His heart went out to the guy.

He knew what it was like to be a man in a difficult situation and be burdened by expectations of unwavering strength and resiliency.

"Max, I need to tell you something." Autumn reached for his hand, which was enough to make him straighten and look her in the eye. "Everything you're feeling is so normal. I have talked dozens of grooms through this moment."

"Really?"

She nodded eagerly and smiled her warm smile. Grey felt the ripples of her generous nature from several feet away. "Absolutely. You'd be surprised. It's always the biggest, strongest guys who have the hardest time with this. And I think I know the reason."

"Why?"

"Because it takes a big heart to be strong. A big heart feels everything." Autumn pointed at his chest. "It doesn't make you weak to be feeling unsure. It only means that you grasp the magnitude of what's happening. This is a big day. You love Katie more than you ever thought it was possible to love someone."

"God yes." Max's voice cracked.

Autumn offered more reassurance with an eager nod. "That's scary. It's like standing outside and looking at the mountains that surround us. You can't even wrap your mind around where so much beauty came from. It seems impossible."

Max exhaled loudly, like he'd been holding his breath. Grey could relate. He, too, felt as though he couldn't breathe. "What do I do?"

"Only you know the answer to that. But I would just

think about what's on the other side of the decision," Autumn said.

"Either I have a life with Katie or I don't."

"Exactly."

"I can't stand the thought of that." Max straightened to his full height, blinked away a tear, and drew a deep breath through his nose. "Wow. I feel so much better. Thank you."

"Of course." Autumn adjusted the boutonniere on his lapel and brushed away a piece of lint. "Any time."

Max looked back down the corridor. "I don't even know where I am. How do I get to where my dad and the groomsmen are?"

Autumn grinned. "Straight down, a left, then a right, and you should be able to find it from there." She patted him on the shoulder. "Now go get married. I'll see you at the reception and we'll have a good laugh over this."

Max smiled, nodded at Grey, then strode down the hall like a new man.

Grey wasn't even sure what to say. "That was spectacular. You are a miracle worker."

"Well, I *am* an armchair psychologist."

"You should charge by the hour."

"I'll take that under advisement. Now let's go check on a million other details."

Autumn started off in the direction Max had gone and Grey went along with her. Of the many things Grey had thought might happen in the course of this wedding, what he'd just witnessed had not been one of them. Autumn was simply amazing.

She also wasn't kidding about the sheer number of

things she had to attend to, all while making herself seemingly invisible. She floated from place to place, checking on flower girl baskets and music. She made sure the mother of the bride had tissues and she retied the bow on the ring bearer's pillow when he nearly lost the bands. She stood at the back during the ceremony, with Grey at her side, observing as everything went off without a hitch. When Max and Katie walked down the aisle, Max winked at her. Autumn returned the sentiment with a thumbs-up.

The ceremony was followed by photographs and then the reception. Grey continued to be astounded by Autumn's attention to the most minuscule and mundane detail, and how she tackled everything in rapid succession. Her job was intense, with an unrelenting pace. There was very little about his career in architecture that he found frenetic. Everything was deliberate. Measured.

When the final guests were wandering out of the ballroom, Grey had to express everything he'd been thinking about the job Autumn had done. "I'm just telling you, whatever money you make, it isn't enough."

She laughed quietly, raising both eyebrows as if to ask if he realized what he was saying. "It's not always like this. Tonight was an extreme case."

"Still, you were amazing." Grey couldn't help but feel like the word was so inadequate. He'd never met any person like her.

"Thank you. I appreciate that." Autumn dug around in her purse and pulled out her keys. "Now it's time to take off these shoes and pass out."

Grey didn't want the evening to end, but she was clearly exhausted and he couldn't think of a reason they should spend any more time together, other than the fact that he wanted to. "Let me walk you to your car." At least this would give them a few minutes alone. Their entire evening had been consumed by other people.

They strolled out of the ballroom, wound their way to the lobby, and then out to the parking lot. The evening air was still warm, but not oppressively humid like a normal North Carolina summer, even up in the mountains. There wasn't much of a breeze either, which meant nature wasn't stirring up the smell of wildflowers or cut grass, leaving Grey to breathe in Autumn's sweet scent.

Autumn stopped at a little silver BMW. "This is me."

Grey was suddenly struck by the urge to hug her goodbye, even when he knew that wasn't appropriate for their working relationship. Instead, he just waved, but he wanted to scream at their circumstances. He couldn't deny his attraction to her. The way he itched to have her in his arms. Kiss her. "Have a good night. Thanks for everything today."

He sensed her hesitation, just as he felt his own restlessness. Desire was stirring inside him. Churning. Telling him to not let her go.

"Okay, then. Good night." Autumn climbed into her car.

Grey waited on the sidewalk for her to leave, disappointment hanging on his shoulders like a weight. She turned the key, but the engine made a clicking sound he knew all too well. She tried it again, but Grey was already sure it wasn't going to work. "Sounds like your battery," he said, walking to her door, which she had opened. He looked around the parking lot. Almost everyone was gone, and it would be strange for them to ask a wedding guest for a jump start. "We could go get my car. Then come back and get yours started. That is if you have jumper cables."

Autumn climbed out. "Nope."

"I doubt I have any. I have a rental car."

Autumn's shoulders dropped. "I'm so tired. I just want to go home and collapse."

Grey spotted one of the resort golf carts nearby. "We'll ride to my cottage and I'll give you a lift back to your place. I can come back and pick you up in the morning if you want."

"Are you sure?" she asked.

For a man who didn't like to get involved in other people's problems, he'd never been more sure of anything in his life. "Absolutely."

Autumn was pretty good at predicting the behavior of others, but she'd never expected that Grey would end up being her knight in shining armor. Not that he wasn't a good man—he was. She simply never would've guessed that he'd go out of his way to demonstrate it.

Back at his cottage, they climbed into his rental car, a sleek black, fully loaded Jaguar. "I had no idea you could rent a car this fancy." She pressed "home" in the navigation app on her phone to guide Grey to her house.

Grey started the engine and the lights flipped on, shining brightly into the dark of night. "It might seem flashy, but it's incredibly safe, too." He checked his mirror, then pulled out onto the access road circling the property.

Autumn remembered Molly talking about the car accident the three brothers had been in when they were teenagers. Reportedly, none of them liked to talk about it, so she didn't bring it up. But she knew that it was a looming presence in everyone's lives, even all these years later. "What do you drive back at home? Or is it too much of a pain to have a car in the city?" Autumn had been to New York many times over the years, but she really only enjoyed visiting for a few days. In general, she preferred places with a big open sky.

"I have a Mercedes I keep in Manhattan. I keep a BMW at my vacation house in Martha's Vineyard." He slid her another glance. "You aren't actually interested in what I drive, are you?"

"Just making conversation." It was the truth. Something about being alone with Grey made her nervous, but excited. They were becoming friends. They were getting closer. It was all good, except that guys like Grey—handsome, capable and smart—were like catnip for Autumn. She might have given Grey a hard time about avoiding temptation, but she needed to do that herself. They were working together. He was practically her boss. More than anything, he still held her future in his hands. "Real East Coast guy, huh?"

"I guess I never really saw the appeal of the west."

"You're so right. All that sunshine. And the beaches. Ugh," she joked.

Grey laughed. "I realize that makes me sound like I never have any fun at all."

Autumn remembered what Molly had said about that. She wondered if most people never got to see the real Grey. Even though he was serious most of the time, she'd seen glimmers of a more relaxed man. She loved those moments. It felt like a challenge to pry them out of him. "What do you do for fun?"

Grey shrugged. "I enjoy chess. I'm a big sports fan. Football. Basketball. I like to swim, too."

"Huh."

"What does that mean?"

Autumn shifted in her seat. "We're very different. Although I like to swim, too."

"See? We have something in common."

Heat bloomed in Autumn's cheeks. He was looking for common ground between them, and it stirred up warm and fuzzy feelings. "Fair warning, I'm more of a lounge by the pool with a margarita sort of girl. Throw in a good book and you'll have to drag me out of there."

He laughed again, but Autumn couldn't help but notice that every time he did it now, it was a little less guarded. More natural. Was she really getting to him the way he was getting to her? Despite everything she'd first thought about working with Grey, she found herself drawn to him like a thirsty bumblebee to sweet, sweet honey. "I didn't expect to say this when we first met, but I like you. I can't say that I know anyone else like you."

Autumn was smiling so wide, she had to turn toward the passenger side window, just so he wouldn't know how damn happy she was. "I like you, too, Grey." *Maybe a little too much.*

"That's nice to hear."

He turned into the main entrance of her neighborhood, Montford, on the North side of Asheville. It was chock-full of beautifully restored historic homes and hosted an eclectic mix of young families, retirees, entrepreneurs and even a few big executives. Grey leaned forward over the steering wheel, peering out at the homes. "Wow. These are some amazing houses."

"Of course. I hadn't really thought about it, but you'd probably love it here during the day. It's got to be heaven for an architect."

"I'm definitely a nerd for old houses." Following the navigation directions, Grey turned into her driveway and killed the engine. "I'll walk you to the door."

"Thanks." Autumn appreciated his gentlemanly ways. It was nice to be treated this way.

They strolled down the front walk and Autumn was trying to figure out a reason to invite him in. Then again, that was a bad idea. He was too good-looking and it would only make her life messier if she opened that door. Still…she was tempted. Every minute in the car with him had chipped away at her resolve to keep things professional.

"I have to ask you something I've been wondering," Grey said when they arrived at the front door. Autumn had forgotten to leave on the outside lights, but the moon was high and full in the sky, casting him in an appealing glow. He really was so handsome. Unfairly so.

"Sure. Ask me anything."

"How do you do what you do after going through a big breakup and a canceled wedding? I don't see how you can stand to be around these happy couples. The reminders are everywhere, aren't they?"

Autumn looked down at the sidewalk for a moment. Funny, but this all made perfect sense to her. "It doesn't make me feel bad to be around people who are in love. If anything, it reminds me of the possibilities. It reminds me that love exists and it's still worth holding out for."

Every bit of his expression, from the half frown to the raised eyebrows, said that he wasn't buying her answer. "So you're not traumatized by everything that happened? It doesn't make you scared?"

"I'm not saying I wasn't hurt. Of course I was. But I'm not scared. It's fine. I'm just busy moving on."

"How is that possible? It's only been a few months, right?"

She understood what Grey was trying to get at, and Molly had taken a similar tack with her, but Autumn didn't want to put her life on hold while she waited for her heart to heal. Sitting around was simply not in her wheelhouse. "It's possible because I've decided that it is. I'm ready to fall in love today. Right now."

"You can't think your way out of this."

"So says the incredibly smart guy who tries to look at every situation analytically."

"I don't think you're over it. Over him. You say you are, but I don't see how you could be."

The light of the moon hit Grey's profile just so, and Autumn was overtaken by an impulse that was impossible to ignore. She wanted to kiss him. She needed her lips all over his, if for no other reason than to prove him wrong. She *was* over her fiancé. Completely. More important, she was alone with an undeniably sexy man on a warm summer night. Everything in her body was saying that a kiss was the only logical conclusion to this conversation. "Maybe you'll see this." She rose up onto her tiptoes, dug her hand into his hair and placed her mouth against his. Her heart was pounding as she waited for him to push her away and tell her no. It would make their work dynamic difficult, but she'd dealt with far worse.

But he didn't do that. He didn't push her away.

Not at all.

To her great surprise, his strong hands gripped her rib cage and he went all-in on the kiss, his lips parting and his tongue teasing hers, sending a flutter of excitement through her. Did he want her like she wanted him? Had he thought about this, too? His reaction made it seem like he had. He wrapped his arms around her waist and pulled her against him. Her chest pressed to his, hips met hips. He was so solid and firm, but there was something surprisingly soft about the kiss. It was gentle. Passionate, but not forceful. But then he slanted his head and took the kiss deeper. That made her rethink the part about passion. He was heat and spark and fire, and even after everything she'd been through, she wanted to be burned.

But then she realized what they were doing. Kissing on her front stoop. Where anyone down on the street could see them. She pulled back, breathless. "We shouldn't be out here."

He gazed down at her, mouth slack and eyes pleading. She took some consolation in the fact that he seemed disappointed. "What? Why?"

"You either have to come inside or go." She squinted and scanned her front yard, but it was dark and her eyesight was terrible.

"I don't understand."

She sighed. "Sometimes people take pictures of me."

"They do?"

"Yes, Grey. To sell."

"Oh." Grey straightened and adopted a posture like he was on high alert, surveying the landscape of her lawn. "Seriously? Like hiding in the bushes?"

"I know. It's crazy, but it happens. They try to catch me doing something terrible like bending over in unflattering sweatpants to pick up a piece of mail I dropped. That actually happened, by the way." That had *not* been a fun day. "It's just part of being my father's daughter. It's gotten a lot worse in the last year. Every new bit of salacious info about my dad brings them out of the woodwork."

"I'd think you would be immune to that here."

"I thought so, too. And I was for the first year or so after I moved. But then people figured out where I live. I even had a tabloid reporter pose as a bride and pretend to be interested in my wedding planning services. They'll do anything."

He returned his attention to her. "I'm so sorry you have to deal with that."

"Thanks."

"Also, for what it's worth, I've seen you bend over and I can't imagine it looking bad."

She playfully hit his arm. "I don't know if I'm supposed to take that as a compliment, but I will." Autumn really wanted to kiss him again, but there was this nagging voice in her head telling her that wasn't wise. She was supposed to be making all three Holloway brothers happy, not just one. "I should probably go inside. I'm exhausted and you have to drive back to Moonlight Ridge. I'm sorry I kissed you. I know I just made things awkward."

"Please don't be sorry. It was nice."

Autumn feared that he was only saying that to be kind to her. He knew how badly she'd been hurt and however cold and analytical he could seem at times, she knew now that there was a feeling man under his hard exterior. His core was thoughtful, and his words were those of a man who was putting her feelings first. "You don't have to make excuses for me. We're working together. You're practically my boss."

He reached down for her hand. "I'm not your boss. And we're only working together until Moonlight Ridge's wedding bookings get on track. I'm helping you."

It still felt as though Autumn had crossed a line she shouldn't have. Even though she'd really wanted to. "I should still probably go inside. Good night, Grey."

He sighed. Whether that was exasperation or frustration, Autumn wasn't sure. "Good night, Autumn. And thank you for today."

Autumn made her way inside, closing the door, then flipping the latch. Her fluffy orange tabby cat, Milton, expressed his disdain for the hours she was keeping. He hadn't been fed. She scooped him up, padded into the kitchen, and filled his food dish. She leaned against the counter, exhausted, the memory of Grey's kiss still humming on her lips. He was a mystery to her, and she still wasn't sure what made him tick, but one thing was undeniable—she wanted more.

Milton finished up his food, and Autumn flipped off the kitchen light, walking back to her bedroom. Just outside her door, her phone beeped with a text.

Be my date to M&M's engagement party Friday?

Autumn grinned at her phone like a fool. The invitation suggested he was just as into that kiss as she'd been. You shouldn't text and drive.

At a red light.

She smiled even wider. I'd love to go.

Perfect. Good night.

Night.

Autumn flopped down on her bed and stared up at the ceiling in the dark. As exhausted as she was, she wouldn't be getting any sleep any time soon. There were too many sexy thoughts of Grey Holloway tumbling around in her head.

# Six

Grey hadn't seen Autumn in days. In fact, it had been all week. It hadn't been his choice, but his more pressing responsibilities had eaten up all his time. The renovations of the brewery had begun, but it was already proving to be a difficult project. The building was old and the contractor was running into problems he hadn't expected. Then there were the still unfinished plans for the new spa, a project that was quickly sliding to the back burner. He had to deal with Opal, the forensic accountant, about the secret audit of Moonlight Ridge, and manage his business in New York from a distance. That last part was becoming a real headache. He was knee-deep in a contentious negotiation to hold on to his most prized employee. In short, he felt like he didn't have a minute to breathe.

That didn't mean he hadn't been thinking about Autumn. Part of the reason he was behind on everything was because he kept finding himself daydreaming about her. It didn't take much to transport him back to that moment when she'd kissed him at her house the other night. She had once again surprised him, but that time, it hadn't been by showing up unannounced or rescuing a wedding. Instead, a kiss. Out of the blue. He'd thought about it several times before that moment, dwelling on the sight of her lips for a few too many heartbeats. But in his head, he'd imagined he would make the first move. Instead, Autumn had broken what little ice was left between them, and the kiss itself had melted it. Every gorgeous feature she possessed was incredible to look at, but even better to touch. And to think, he'd only had a taste. When she'd talked to him about temptation the first day they met, he was convinced he could resist anything. Now he knew that Autumn was poised to become his biggest weakness.

To make up for his absence all week, he'd invited Autumn to come over a half hour before Mack and Molly's engagement party. He wanted the chance to enjoy a glass of wine with her before heading over. Even though he'd worked for much of the day, it had been a beautiful day for July Fourth and he hoped for an even nicer evening, complete with fireworks over the lake. If he was lucky, there might even be a few fireworks with Autumn. But he didn't want to get ahead of himself.

He rushed outside as soon as he heard her car door, arriving in time to see her rising up out of her silver BMW. She was wearing yet another dress apparently designed to knock the breath out of him. Again it was lace, but this one was red, and unlike the one she'd worn to the wedding last weekend, it had skinny straps that showed off her lovely shoulders and shimmery skin. As she got closer, his eyes were drawn to the sexy neckline, which dipped low between the swell of her breasts. The sight made everything in his body run hot.

He greeted her at the end of the driveway, gently gripping her elbow and loving the silkiness of her skin. "You look absolutely beautiful." He kissed her cheek and breathed in her sweet scent, the perfect complement to the aroma of wildflowers already in the air.

She grinned at him. "What happened to not laying it on too thick?"

Grey wanted to kick himself for the stupid comment he'd made in her office the other day. "I was trying to be professional. But now that we're not on the clock, I don't see any reason why I can't say that you and that dress are a knockout."

"You look pretty amazing, too, just so you know." She eyed him up and down in a way that made his chest squeeze tight. Was she thinking what he was thinking? That they needed to explore everything that logically came after a kiss? Clothes being cast aside and hands skimming over bare skin? Just the thought of that moment with Autumn had him ready to jettison every plan and obligation he had. If it wasn't his own brother's engagement party tonight, he would have canceled without a second thought.

"Thank you. How's your car running?" They made

their way across to the patio where he'd left out a chilled bottle of white wine and two glasses.

"Great. You were right. It was the battery. Quick fix."

"I would've gladly come to pick you up that next morning."

"I used a ride app. I didn't want to interrupt your push-up schedule."

He laughed as he opened the wine bottle and poured two glasses, handing her one before taking his own. "To many more weddings at Moonlight Ridge."

"The most ironic toast in the world considering the person making it. But I still like it. Cheers." She clinked her glass with his and took a sip. "Mmm. Delicious."

There was something so sexy about the way she reveled in everything—food, wine, the world. She was so much better at living in the moment than he was. "I'm so sorry about not seeing you this week. I've been incredibly busy."

"It's okay. I was super busy, too." She peered up at him, managing to put him on notice with the warmest brown eyes he'd ever seen. "Of course, it did make me second-guess what happened in front of my house the other night. A week of you being so busy that you couldn't pop by my office isn't a great reaction to a kiss."

"I really was busy. It wasn't a line."

"And I was super busy, too. It doesn't mean I didn't have a spare ten minutes in there to say hello or catch up."

He was officially an idiot. Grey hadn't really thought

through how Autumn would react to his absence. "Oh, God. I'm sorry. That's not what happened. I swear."

"I'll take your word for it." She took another sip of her wine, seeming unconvinced.

"I wouldn't have invited you for a glass of wine if I hadn't enjoyed the kiss. You were the one who stopped it."

"I was being careful. I wanted to preserve your privacy. It's not fun being in the spotlight I occasionally find myself in."

He hated that she had to live like that. He hated that she would ever question herself, or his own inclination to spend time with her. "Let me prove it to you." He set his wineglass on the table and placed his hand on her jaw, his fingers sliding along the side of her graceful neck. His other hand landed on her hip, the lace fabric silky under his touch while her warmth radiated into his skin. She gazed up at him, seeming amused, a smile playing at the corner of her tempting lips. As much as he wanted to drink in her beauty, he also wanted to immerse himself in the kiss. So he let his eyes drift shut as his lips met hers. For a guy who had a hard time turning off his brain, every thought he had blurred. Her lips were so soft, her hair so silky as he dug his fingers into it, her tongue so sweet and hot. With every second that ticked by, their bodies pressed against each other harder, the kiss became more urgent, and the pressure of his need for her got a little more impossible to bear.

But once again, she was the one to put on the brakes. "Grey. We're going to be late. A few more seconds of kissing you and clothes are going to start coming off."

Even though the kiss had ended, they were still in each other's arms, breathing hard, the attraction between them charging the thick summer air like a thunderstorm was brewing.

"I fail to see a problem with that."

A quiet laugh left her lips, which were even more full after their kiss. "You're bad."

"I can be, if that's what you want."

She cocked an eyebrow at him. "Technically, we're still working together."

He shook his head. "I've been thinking about that. After seeing everything you did last weekend at that wedding, I'm convinced you don't need any help unless you want it." Grey had already planned to tell Mack as much this evening. The idea of anyone keeping tabs on Autumn was ridiculous. She had everything in hand.

"I do like having you around. You make my job more fun." She bit down on her lip, making his thoughts go fuzzy again.

"How about this? From now on, I will pester you purely on a volunteer basis."

She shrugged. "I liked it when you felt accountable."

"No, you did not. You hated the idea of me interfering."

She took another sip of her wine. "That was before we became friends."

Grey couldn't contain the smile that crossed his face. He realized then that almost every minute of fun he'd had since he returned to Asheville had been with Autumn. He loved spending time with his family, but there was always a layer of tension. Between the trouble with the business and Jameson's recovery, there were very few easy conversations. Autumn challenged him, but when she did, it was just about getting to the heart of the matter. And with her, everything was simply more enjoyable.

"I'd still like to remove any constraints of a work relationship." He drew in a breath, preparing himself for what he was about to say next. "Especially if it's going to prevent us from getting to know each other on a more personal basis."

Autumn drifted into him, placing her hand on his chest. "Are you saying you want to see what comes after the next kiss?"

He swallowed hard. He loved her honesty, even when it put everything on the line. "In a word, yes."

She brushed the lapel of his jacket and smiled. "Let's play it by ear. We can start by getting to this engagement party."

Jameson Holloway loved having his family around him. He only wished he could keep up with them. "Can I do anything to help?" he asked as Molly, bride-to-be and his future daughter-in-law, whizzed past him. Jameson had been parked in an Adirondack chair out on his patio by his nurse, Giada, the woman driving him to distraction on a daily basis. He was under strict orders to relax. How was he supposed to do that while everyone else was busy with last-minute preparations for Mack and Molly's engagement party? He'd waited for years for a moment like this, and he'd been sidelined. "Seriously. I'd like to do something here," he called out to anyone who would listen.

Molly bustled over to him. It was an amazing thing that her curly hair always kept moving even after she'd come to a stop. "You know Giada wants you to stay put. This is a lot of excitement, and the party is set to last for several hours. You want to keep your strength, don't you?"

Jameson deeply appreciated how much those around him cared for him. He only wished it didn't feel so damn patronizing. His recovery was taking too long and going too slow for his liking. He didn't want to sit in a chair while life went on around him. "Yes and no," he answered. "More than anything, I'd like to feel like I'm a part of this."

Molly leaned down and kissed him on the cheek. "You're the reason we're all here, and I think you know that."

Jameson peered up into Molly's pretty face. He couldn't wait until she was his daughter-in-law, but in so many ways, she'd seemed like his daughter for years. "No, no. This is your night. Mack's night. It's not about me." He realized then that he was being an insufferable old man. This wasn't about him. And he needed to stop dwelling on what he wanted.

"Can I get you anything?" Molly asked. "I'm heading back inside. Guests are arriving. Grey and Autumn just got here."

*Grey and Autumn?* Jameson couldn't help but wonder about that particular combination. "Can you send

Mack and Grey out? I'd love to catch up with them both before things get too busy."

"Will do."

Molly disappeared through the side door of the house, passing Giada as she came outside. In a maddening blue dress that hugged every inch of her voluptuous form, Giada was the real reason he couldn't relax. Every time she came into view, he could feel his blood pressure rising. Her presence made him feel the glorious frustration of youth, when you know who you want and your body runs hot and you don't think you can wait another minute.

Giada looked over at him and smiled, although a grin from Giada always came with a thick layer of skepticism. She was always watching, waiting for him to do something he wasn't supposed to do, like smoking a cigar. Or have any fun at all. It was one of the cruel twists in his life that the only woman he wanted to take to bed, the woman who most made him feel alive, was also the person charged with reminding him of his limitations. This was not a formula for romance and Jameson could admit that at this point in his life, he wanted that. Giada was perfect for him. They were only six years apart in age, they kept each other on their toes, and she stoked the fire in him like no other.

Giada slid him another glance and he managed to catch her with his gaze, or at least that was what he told himself when she traipsed over to him. "How are you doing over here? Ready to make a break for it?"

"Why did you make me sit in this particular chair?

Even with my cane, there's no way I can get out of this thing on my own."

Giada perched on the edge of the chair next to him, crossing her legs, which made the slit at the front of her dress fall open. She was quick to close it up, but he still happily stole a glimpse of her inner thigh. "Exactly why I put you here. I want you to stay put. You're the patriarch. Let people come to you."

Jameson wasn't sure about all of that. All he could think was that he wanted to hold her hand. He wanted to kiss her. He wanted to be his old self and take her to dinner, dance with her under a starry sky on a night like tonight, then make love to her for hours. "I'd like to go for a walk later tonight. After this winds down. After the fireworks."

"Let's see how you feel after the party."

He reached over for her hand. Very little fazed her, but she did look at him like he was crazy for making such a public display of affection. "I want to be alone with you, Giada. Is that so hard for you to understand?"

"You're alone with me all the time."

"But not like this. It's a warm summer night, the stars are about to come out, and my son is getting married. It makes a man feel romantic." He rubbed the back of her hand with his thumb. "I want to kiss you. I want to do a lot more than kiss you."

"I will promise you a walk. As for the rest of it, we'll see."

Mack and Grey emerged from the side door, headed straight for the spot where Jameson and Giada were sitting. Giada pulled her hand back and popped up out of her chair, smoothing the front of her dress. Jameson didn't enjoy the fact that their conversation had been cut short, but she hadn't shut him down completely. This was progress.

"Mack. Grey," Giada said, giving them each a quick hug. "I need to do a few more things inside. Will you spend some time with your father?"

"That's exactly who we came out to see," Mack answered, taking the seat Giada had just vacated.

"Perfect." Giada peered down at Jameson with a look that made him wonder if he might be lucky enough to get more than one kiss from her later. "I'll be back in a little bit."

"Don't stay away too long." Jameson watched as she walked away, the sway of her hips pure poetry.

"How are you feeling, Pops?" Grey asked.

"Great. Amazing." He looked over at Mack, who simply seemed different since he'd finally proposed to Molly and put that ring on her finger. He was more at ease with everything, although there was still determination simmering in him. He'd really taken the business of Moonlight Ridge by the horns. "Mack's about to get married and you're both here. If we just had Travis, it would've made everything perfect. Hopefully that will happen in good time."

"There was just no way for him to get away. Between his restaurant opening in LA and working as a mentor on that cooking show, he's stretched to the limit. He promised he'll be here for the wedding," Mack said. "And if he goes back on that one, I'll never forgive him."

Jameson knew that Mack was merely making a joke, but the idea of any of his sons not forgiving the other for anything didn't sit right with him. The boys had done a lot of finger-pointing after the accident that tore their entire family apart. Jameson understood how much of that had been a product of their youth, and letting their stubborn egos stand in the way, but it still didn't make him any less sad about the years that had been lost. The years when the three of them went their separate ways.

"He'll be here," Grey said. "You know he wanted to be here tonight. If anyone should understand how hard it is to step away from work, it should be you, Mack."

"Don't act like I'm the only workaholic. You're just as bad," Mack said. "Did you even leave your cottage all week?"

"I did. To do site visits for *your* brewery," Grey said.

Jameson had made a point of raising three hard-working sons, but he hadn't realized how much that might just backfire on him. Mack, Grey and Travis had taken it to the extreme, pouring everything into their careers and leaving love and family on the periphery. Aside from making a full recovery and romancing Giada, Jameson's other chief goal in life was to make sure all three of his sons figured out that there was so much more to life than work. He couldn't stand to watch them be so bullheaded about it. "Listen, you two. I know Travis isn't here, but I'd still like us to get back to regular Sunday family lunches. We've talked about it, but I want us to actually make it happen. Giada has said she'll cook."

"That'll be a big upgrade," Mack quipped.

"Not all of my cooking is terrible," Jameson sniped back.

"No need to get defensive, Pops, just because you aren't a great chef. We know you always did your best," Grey said.

"You two still haven't answered me," Jameson said. "Can we start this Sunday?"

Grey and Mack exchanged looks, then Grey answered, "It might not be this week. I might have to head back to New York for a few days. I won't be long."

"You didn't tell me about this." Mack made zero effort to hide his annoyance. Then again, he was shouldering a lot of responsibility at Moonlight Ridge.

"I don't know yet. We're renegotiating the employment agreement for one of my staff architects. She's being pursued by another firm and she's one of the most important members of our team, so it's getting dicey." Grey turned to Jameson. "But I promise we can do it the week after. One of us will coordinate with Giada."

Jameson smiled. That was all he'd wanted to hear. All he needed was a cigar and this could shape up to be a perfect night. "Excellent."

From inside the house came a clamor of voices. "Sounds like the guests are pouring in," Mack said, getting up from his seat. "I should find Molly so we can greet everyone together."

"Yes. Go," Grey said, seeming preoccupied. He'd always been a big thinker, very insular even when he'd been young.

"Everything all right, son?" Jameson asked after Mack had left.

"Yes. Absolutely. Everything's great." Grey offered an unconvincing smile.

Just then, Autumn stepped out onto the patio. In a showstopper of a dress, she scanned the area, her face lighting up when she spotted Grey. She beelined over to them.

"There you are," he said as he got up from his seat.

Perhaps it was that Jameson's radar for romance was on high alert, but he couldn't ignore the tone in Grey's voice, or the abrupt change in his demeanor. Grey was practiced in hiding his true feelings when it came to most things, but Jameson knew his son. If he'd had to put money on it, he would've bet that Grey was smitten with Ms. Kincaid. Jameson had never seen him like this before. And he couldn't have been happier about it.

"Hi, Mr. Holloway," Autumn said, offering her hand.

"It's nice to see you," Jameson said as he returned the gesture.

"You, too, sir. I'm very excited for Molly and Mack." She looked up at the sky, which was quickly filling with stars. "They got a beautiful night to celebrate, didn't they?"

"Your family really is lovely," Autumn said as she and Grey went off in search of a drink. "Your dad is so great."

He placed his hand at the center of her back when they reached the bar at the far end of the patio. Just that one touch sent shivers of anticipation through her. She'd legitimately worried all week that Grey simply wasn't interested. After that kiss back at his cottage, she knew that wasn't the case. And she couldn't wait to see if he might want to kiss her some more after they got back.

"What do you want to drink?" he asked.

"White wine is good."

"Two please." Grey stuffed a large bill in the tip jar.

"You didn't say anything when I told you that your family is lovely."

Grey took the two glasses and handed her one. "Oh, yeah. I agree, but believe me, we have our problems."

They wandered away to a quiet spot at the back corner of the sprawling multilevel stone patio. Much like Grey's cottage, the view from Jameson's house had a view of the lake, but it wasn't quite as secluded. It was more a showpiece on the hill for everyone to admire. All around them, candles flickered as the sky darkened and people mingled. Happy chatter mixed with soft music. Love was in the air. "Every family has problems, Grey."

He took a sip of his wine. "I suppose. I only know that everything is difficult and messy with my brothers now. It's been like that for more than a decade, but it wasn't always like that."

She could guess what he was talking about, but she hadn't had the courage to ask about it before. "The accident? Was that the start of it?"

His eyes flashed with intensity that she wasn't sure how to read. Was it anger? Was it betrayal? "You know about that?"

"Molly told me. It made such a huge impression on

her. That was when she and Mack first fell in love but they were so young. I don't think she knew how to handle it at the time."

"And Mack took off immediately without saying a word to her..." Grey's voice drifted off much the way Molly's had when she'd first shared the story with Autumn.

"It's not an easy thing what you three went through. Physically and mentally."

"Is this another armchair psychologist session?"

He could be so stubborn. So closed off. "I'm just sympathizing with what you went through."

Grey sighed, seeming exasperated. "I don't have a right to dwell on it or complain. Travis suffered the most. He's the one who paid the biggest price. He lost his dreams that night."

"Because he couldn't play football anymore?" By all accounts, Travis had been an incredibly talented player with a big future ahead of him.

"That was the aftereffect, but he nearly died, too. It was horrible." Grey nodded in Jameson's direction. "It was all-consuming for our dad."

"But surely it took its toll on you, too. Just like it did on Mack."

He looked down at the ground, seeming introspective. She didn't want to make things too heavy tonight, but she did want him to realize that he might be minimizing his own pain. "It taught me to never lose my cool. I did that night and it's always stuck with me. That moment when I let go of all logical thought and gave in to my emotions. I don't like to think about it."

Autumn heard the agony in Grey's voice, even when he was still retaining his usual calm and even exterior. No wonder he was always reserved. No wonder he had so much self-discipline. She wasn't sure what he'd been like before that fateful night, but she was fairly certain that the accident had changed him. At least on some level. He saw his emotions and a lack of self-control as his contribution to the accident, and he seemed determined to never repeat the mistake.

In the center of the patio, Mack and Molly stood together, Molly clinking on a wineglass with a piece of flatware. "If I can steal everyone's attention for a minute," Molly said, holding up a finger. "I want to thank you all for joining us tonight to celebrate our engagement. Mack and I are very happy to share this exciting time in our lives with you."

"I'd like to propose a toast," Mack said, directing his attention to Molly. "To the most beautiful woman in the world. Thank you for saying yes when I gave you a million reasons to say no."

Everyone laughed, and someone in the crowd shouted, "Hear, hear!" Autumn and Grey clapped as they watched Mack and Molly get lost in a kiss.

When Molly came up for air, her cheeks were flame red. "That's all. Tonight is for fun, so I hope that you will eat, drink, dance and be merry."

A crowd of guests closed in on Mack and Molly, offering congratulations.

"I guess we can save our good wishes for later," Autumn said.

Grey picked up his wineglass and downed the last

of it. "Let's grab our chance to get another drink while everyone is distracted by the happy couple."

Autumn and Grey returned to the bar to fetch two more glasses of wine, then found a pair of chairs where they could sit and talk. "I have to ask," Grey said.

"Uh-oh. The last time you started a line like that, you asked me fifty questions about my ex and whether or not I was over him."

Grey looked at her with soft eyes. "I'm sorry. I can keep my mouth shut if you'd prefer."

One mention of his mouth and she was stuck on the memories of the two times they'd kissed. Would he want more from her tonight? Was that a good idea? Her body was completely on board, but her brain was only 95 percent convinced. She knew how Grey felt about romance. She knew that he didn't take love seriously. *Your fiancé dumped you. Have some fun.* "No. I'm fine. You can ask me anything."

"You said you can handle seeing strangers be happy and in love, but is it hard for you to see your best friend in that situation? Getting engaged and planning a wedding?"

She drew in a deep breath through her nose. It was as if he'd been listening in on the thoughts she'd just been having. "I wouldn't say it bothers me. I love Molly like a sister and I couldn't be any happier for her."

"But? I sense a *but* somewhere in there…"

"Well, remember when I said that the weddings don't bother me?"

"I do. Mostly because I can't believe you still feel like that." He took another drink of his wine.

"That's because that's my career, and that is incredibly important to me, but it's also work. In a situation like this, where it's just about everyone gathering and celebrating, I do get a little misty-eyed. They're mostly happy tears for Molly and Mack, but there's a bittersweet edge to it. Thinking about what could have been."

He nodded slowly. "You let down your guard. And that's when you can't think your way out of it."

She took a moment to let his words tumble around in her head. "I guess there's only so much I can compartmentalize."

"If it helps at all, and I'm not sure it will, I want you to know that I'm amazed by the way you roll with everything. You don't let things get to you."

She narrowed her sights on him. She loved the way he liked to dissect a situation. He'd called her an armchair psychologist, but he was just as immersed in the practice as she was. "It's not that it doesn't affect me, Grey. It's that no matter what happens, I try to stay positive. Molly's happiness is a reminder that it's out there for everyone. It doesn't mean it's less likely for me."

Just then, the music was turned up a notch or two and Mack and Molly started a slow dance on the uppermost level of the patio. Above them, string lights were looped back and forth, casting a soft romantic glow. Everyone stood and watched. Autumn truly was happy for her best friend. Her love story with Mack had been hard-fought. But Autumn couldn't deny that she wanted what Molly had found, and she didn't like to think about how long she might have to wait to fall in love again.

Autumn was about to wipe away a tear when Grey surprised her. He took her hand. Her heart fluttered with anticipation, the thrill of the unknown. The rest of her felt like she might melt into a puddle. Then he rubbed the back of her hand with his thumb. Gently. Softly. And unless she was reading the situation completely wrong, there was a message behind it. It stirred up so much heat in her that it felt like foreplay. Her more salient thoughts about love and romance and what she wanted were set aside in favor of more immediate needs. His touch. His kiss. More than a taste of what was brewing between them.

After one song, others joined Mack and Molly up on the dance floor. Even Jameson made his way out there with Giada.

Grey tugged on Autumn's hand. "Come on."

She wasn't so sure. It was one of the only times in recent memory when she'd hesitated. It was one thing to stand in the shadows and have Grey quietly hold her hand. It was another to dance in front of his family. The Holloways were her employers and they'd essentially put her on probation when they'd asked Grey to oversee the job she was doing. "Are you sure?"

"I am." Grey walked her to the dance floor, then possessively pulled her into his arms the instant they were there. He held her tight against him, his hand flat in the small of her back.

She could do nothing but surrender to the moment and his actions. Nothing else felt right. She drew in his warm smell and drank up the feeling of being in his arms. Autumn couldn't help but notice that Mack had caught what was going on. "Your brother is watching us."

Grey pulled her even closer and turned them until his back was to Mack and Molly. "Let him."

"Grey, your dad is my employer. And that's not a small thing. Being a wedding planner is incredibly important to me and I've been on thin ice, even if everyone was tiptoeing around the issue." Her job anchored her to the life she had here in Asheville. It was the most settled she'd felt in her entire life. It was the one place where she felt like she could breathe. And she still felt that way, even after being dumped right before her wedding.

"I understand. My career is incredibly important to me, too."

Autumn decided that there was nothing wrong with a dance, even when there was zero space between their bodies. Even when they'd kissed before they'd come to the party and she was hoping like anything that they could return to his cottage together. As if she needed much pushing in that direction, Grey nuzzled her hair with his nose. It made her knees weak. It made her want to close her eyes and bow into him.

"There's no crime in dancing," he muttered straight into her ear. His breath was warm against her skin, so hot that it stood out against the balmy night air.

"Absolutely true." She really liked this version of Grey, the one who threw at least a little bit of caution to the wind. He was endlessly appealing. But as badly as she wanted him, there was still a tug of uncertainty inside her. She knew that she was over her ex, but seeing Molly get engaged was starting to make her realize that she might not be over what had happened. She might not be over the sting of the ultimate rejection, when someone has taken you to the brink of a lifetime commitment, only to tell you that you're not worth it.

To make things more complicated, between Grey's physical presence and their conversation, he was stirring up a million thoughts in her head. "You know, I feel like I need to apologize to you."

"For what?" He pulled his head back and looked down at her. His eyes were dark in the low light, steeped with intensity.

"The first day we met. When I said that I'd figured you out. Clearly I hadn't. I mean, I haven't. There's a lot to unpack with you, Grey."

He granted her a fraction of a smile. "I could say the same thing about you."

Autumn shrugged. "Maybe. But I'm not sure it's quite the same. I'm a pretty open book."

"And you think I'm not open?"

"I didn't say that. I just think there's far more to you than your handsome, capable exterior."

He grinned a little wider, then pulled her closer, whispering into her ear. "You say things like that and it just makes me want to leave with you. It makes me want to walk you back to my place and be alone with you. It makes me want to pull off this maddening dress and make you forget about the things other people think we should or shouldn't do."

Autumn swallowed hard, finding it difficult to get

back the lump in her throat. Desire welled up inside her, flooding her brain and her body. She no longer merely wanted Grey. She needed him. "Yes. I want that, too."

# Seven

Autumn had always loved fireworks on the Fourth of July. This year, they were a pain in her butt. Everyone would notice if she and Grey left the party before they had taken place.

"Grey. We can't leave now. Everyone will notice."

He grimaced. "I really don't think they will. We'll sneak around the side. No one will miss us."

Autumn didn't like the idea of this plan, but she was fighting some physical urges that were becoming quite potent. Plus, she appreciated that Grey wanted to break a few rules. "Okay. Let's go."

Grey took her hand and they slipped around the back corner of the house and stole off into the night, across the green grass until they reached the path that wound through Moonlight Ridge. It wasn't walking—it was

faster than that, but it didn't feel like running, either.
It was more that they arrived at his door with Autumn
having little recollection of her feet ever having hit the
ground.

Once inside Autumn tossed aside her clutch handbag, unsure of where it landed. It was like an out-of-
body experience when he kissed her, except that she
was keenly aware of how much longing was built up
inside her. She ached for him. She craved his touch,
everywhere, as fast *and* as slow as he wanted to go.
She wanted the full experience of being with Grey.
She wanted to jump into the deepest part of the ocean
and not come up for air until her lungs were burning.

Their hands were all over each other. Autumn's fingers dug into his biceps, frustrated by his suit jacket, but
too focused on the kiss to do anything about it. Their
mouths were hungry for more as their tongues wound
together in an endless circle. Somehow they ended up
in the kitchen, probably because it was so close to the
front door. He pressed Autumn hard against the stone
countertop, sending a shock wave of pain through her,
a delicious contrast to the sheer heaven of Grey's kiss.
He reached behind her and drew down the zipper of her
dress, slipping his hand inside to her bare skin. Having
his skin against hers like that was another jolt to the
system. She wanted more. She needed it.

She threaded her hands inside his jacket and pushed
it down onto the floor, then went for the buttons on his
shirt. His lips were on hers again, his tongue toying
with hers while he reached down for the hem of her
dress, pulling it up to midthigh. That gave her enough

freedom of movement to wrap her leg around his hip and muscle him closer.

Grey growled into her mouth once she'd freed him from his shirt and began exploring the hard planes of his back, and the rocky perfection of his shoulders. She felt every push-up, every muscle carved and defined, just begging to be explored and appreciated. She was desperate to have a good look, but her glasses were fogging up, and honestly they were just getting in the way.

"I need to take off my glasses." She removed them and set them on the kitchen counter.

"I noticed that you wore them tonight. I like it. A lot." His eyes were dark with desire, his lips slack from breathing too hard. "But what you really need to take off is this dress."

He turned her around until she was facing the kitchen cabinets, slipping his hands under the skinny straps of her dress and letting it puddle to the floor. The rush of cooler air to her skin was a welcome respite to the heat she'd been enduring, but it also shook awake every nerve ending in her body. Every inch of her was now fully engaged in the business of needing Grey.

He unhooked her bra and dropped it into the growing pile of clothes on the floor. He pressed the full length of his body against her back, reaching around front to cup and caress her breasts, his thumbs rolling over the top of her hard nipples. He kissed her neck and Autumn dropped her head to one side to grant him greater access as he dotted her shoulder with wet hot kisses.

"Tell me what you like, Autumn," he said into her ear before taking a gentle nip of her lobe.

She had no idea how to put it into words. For her, it wasn't about an act or touching her in a particular spot. She needed to feel worshipped. Adored. Before she could answer, Grey slid his hand down her belly and into the front of her panties. He moved his fingers against her center in steady circles, making the pressure between her legs build. "That's the perfect place to start," she muttered. She closed her eyes and soaked up the sensations, the way everything he did was so right on time. The way everything he said set her world on fire.

Autumn felt the peak closing in, her body getting fitful and eager for her reward. Grey molded his one hand around her breast while the other continued to send her barreling toward the cliff. As she gasped, the pleasure rolled over her in fast pulses. Again and again, until it faded into a pleasant hum. It was a start, and a beautiful one at that, but she wanted so much more.

She turned in Grey's arms and kissed him with abandon, digging the fingers of both hands into his thick hair. Cupping the back of his head, she pulled him deeper into their kiss. She wanted to be one with him, and this was a step in that direction. She slipped her knee between his legs and ground it against him. Even through his pants she could feel how hard he was. She couldn't wait to have him in her hand. In her mouth.

As if Grey understood what she was thinking, he took her hand and led her to the room she'd only peeked inside before—his bedroom. As soon as they crossed the threshold, she unbuttoned and unzipped his pants, pushing them to the floor. Grey steered her to the bed, easing her back on to the mattress. He gripped her rib cage, caressing the undersides of her breasts with his thumbs, all while making her feel as though he could see right into her soul. He had such a penetrating stare, and she already knew how much was behind those stunning eyes. It made her feel seen in a way she'd never been more.

Peeling down her panties and wriggling them past her hips, she was finally naked. She was his. Their gazes connected again. He had that serious look again, the one he wore nearly all the time. This time, she was happy for it. She wanted him to take this charge with all the gravity it deserved. He drew a finger up the center of her thigh, from her knee and heading toward her center. He inched along, all the while studying her face and making her squirm in her own skin. When he reached her apex, she bucked at his touch, even though she'd experienced it moments earlier. It all felt new again.

Autumn scooted back on the bed and with the curl of a finger, invited him to join her. As soon as his long body was next to hers, she rolled to her side, facing him. She tugged down his boxer briefs, then took his length in her hand. He was magnificent. That was the only way to say it. Did Grey have any shortcomings at all? She didn't think so. As she took long strokes with her hand, he growled like an animal into her ear. She loved hearing him make such a declaration of what he liked, even if it came without words.

"Please tell me you have a condom," she whispered into his ear.

"I do. I'll get it in a minute."

She pushed him to his back and shifted on to her knees between his legs. She lowered her head and huffed warm air against his length. Grey groaned again and thrashed his head back and forth on the mattress. If he thought that felt good, he was going to be over the moon for what came next. She wrapped her fingers around him again, taking long passes with her hand, rolling her thumb over the tip every time. She then lowered her head and took him into her mouth. The delicate nature of this moment could not be overstated—she had him at her mercy and he was giving in to it completely. He dug his fingers into her hair and gently massaged her scalp as she let her lips glide along his length, and let her tongue apply the extra pressure.

His breaths were coming quick, the strokes of his fingers going faster. "Autumn, I'm going to come and I don't want to. I want to make love to you."

Just hearing him say the words brought her mind to the immensity of the moment. She hadn't done this in some time, and the last person hadn't taken very good care of her heart. Still, she felt safe with Grey. He might not be built for love, but at least he'd been honest with her about it.

He sat up and opened the drawer of the bedside table, pulling out the foil pouch, tearing it open and rolling it on. Autumn shifted to her back and scooted to the center of the mattress while Grey crawled over to her in pursuit. The anticipation made her feel nothing less than totally open to him, and she let her knees fall to the bed. She wanted him. Now.

He came inside, sinking into her, inch by blissful

inch. He took long and forceful thrusts, but he also wasn't in a hurry. Every move he made was intentional. Deliberate. Just like Grey—focused. She'd always been a romantic and she expected a moment when she'd become fuzzy-headed and the world around her would seem to disappear. But that didn't happen with Grey. Every thrust he made kept her in the here and now, but she was still immersed in unimaginable pleasure. It was a mind-blowing experience. Sex had never felt like this before.

She tilted her hips to be closer to him and that left his pelvic bone to press against her center. The sensation became even more intense—he filled her so perfectly, moved inside her like they were made to be together. He kissed her deeply, but with so much tenderness she found it hard to breathe. And in that moment, she feared what might happen if she and Grey made love more than once. She was the woman most prone to falling. And Grey was a little too close to perfect.

It wasn't like Grey had been completely starved for sex, but it had been awhile since a woman had been in his bed. Work and career were always getting in the way. But he was questioning whether he remembered how this went. Autumn was unlike any woman he'd ever been with. She said things with her body that made him question whether she was real. She was like a fantasy brought to life, lush and beautiful and so worth savoring.

"You feel so good," she said breathlessly. "I'm so

close." She pulled her knees higher, allowing him to sink even deeper inside her.

He grappled with how good it felt to have her tighten around him. It made his head swim, his consciousness dip and sway. He pressed his lips against her sweet and sexy mouth, the one he never wanted to stop kissing. The tension was doubling in his hips as her hands traveled across his back and her ankles rubbed against his butt. Every thrust was taking him closer to the edge, and he felt her gathering around him. She was tightening, coiling, holding on. The pressure was becoming impossible to endure. He was about to give way at any second. Her breaths were short. His were, too. They were in sync. In every way.

Autumn came first, calling out and knocking her head back. He let go the instant she did, the orgasm so intense that his mind went blank, then shifted to a kaleidoscope of colors. He lowered himself and she immediately nestled her face in his neck, kissing his skin with her warm lips. Grey rolled onto the bed, holding her close. The weight of the moment sat squarely on his shoulders. She had crossed a line with him that he'd been worried she wasn't ready for. He'd let his own desire get in the way. Yes, she'd been an eager participant, but it still didn't make him any less concerned.

"You okay?" he asked, gently caressing her back.

"Are you kidding me? That was amazing." He felt her smile between them when she kissed him softly.

"It really was."

She curled closer to him, hitching her leg over his.

"You're not nearly as much of a grump as people told me you were."

Grey had to laugh. He knew he had that reputation. It didn't bother him. His seriousness had served him well. It had kept him on a narrow path, where life was stable and predictable and that was exactly the way he liked it. Out of the corner of his eye, Grey saw flashes of light in the sky. He pointed at the window. "Look. The fireworks."

"Oh, good. We don't have to miss them after all."

He kissed the top of Autumn's head and they watched the show in silence—every color of the rainbow glittering against the dark sky. When it was over, Grey was about to say something when he heard how slow and even Autumn's breaths had become. Her head was heavy on his arm. She was asleep. And he was right on the brink.

Grey slept like a baby, but he woke up far earlier than he wanted to on a Saturday, especially on a holiday weekend. Perhaps it was his conscience shaking him awake. Last night with Autumn had been incredible, but he'd been well aware that he was walking into a messy and complicated situation with her and he'd done it anyway. That didn't sit well with him. He avoided complications. He didn't pursue them. The fact that it all revolved around the state of Autumn's heart made the stakes a little too high for him. He could stay detached, but could she?

She stirred in bed, rolling from her back to her side and snuggling the covers up to her chin. Her hair was mussed and she had a blissful look on her face as she drifted back to sleep. She was so sexy and beautiful it was hard for him to wrap his head around it. He sincerely hoped that everything she'd said last night was true. That she was fine with the idea of keeping things casual and just having fun, but he wasn't convinced, and only time would tell.

From the other room, his cell phone rang. He leapt out of bed and dashed into the kitchen, where he'd left his phone on the counter. He answered without looking at the Caller ID.

"Mr. Holloway, good morning. I'm sorry for calling so early." It was his executive assistant, Ryan Valdez.

"Ryan, what's up?" It was a little after 8:00 o'clock on a Saturday morning, so this was indeed an unusual time to hear from him.

"I came into the office this morning to catch up on some work, and Ms. Keller's office is empty."

Grey felt his body go cold. Vivian Keller was the most talented architect on his team, and clients loved her. But the negotiation to renew her employment agreement had been going poorly. Now Grey knew that it had fallen apart. "Wow. Okay." His mind was a flurry of activity. Vivian was the lead on multiple projects and they were already short one architect on staff after someone else had taken leave to care for a sick relative.

"I know the timing is terrible. I've tried to get ahold of the legal team to find out what happened with the negotiations, but nobody's answering their phone. Ms. Keller won't pick up either."

"It's a holiday weekend. I'm guessing nobody wants

to deal with it." Grey leaned against the kitchen counter, drawing a deep breath in through his nose. "Ryan, you should be enjoying your weekend, not working."

He laughed. "I'm just following your lead, Mr. Holloway. It's not like you weren't spending plenty of weekends here before you went to North Carolina."

"But I'm the boss. I don't really have a choice."

"Some people might say that because you're the boss, you always have a choice."

Grey hadn't really thought about it like that. He wasn't sure he could ever give up that much control. "I guess I need to get my butt on a plane and head home."

"Obviously, that's your call, Mr. Holloway, but it's only a matter of time before one of the other architects gets wind of Vivian leaving. With the number of projects we're juggling right now, it could be mayhem in the office on Monday morning if you're not here."

If anyone knew the climate of Grey's firm, it was Ryan. If he expected mayhem, Grey didn't doubt it. Grey sighed. He could hardly believe this bit of bad luck, but he didn't have a choice. He had to deal with it. "You're right. Can you get me on a flight for later today?"

"I'm sure it won't be a problem. I don't think the 5th of July is a big travel day."

"Especially when it's on a Saturday." Out of the corner of his eye, Grey spotted Autumn in the doorway to his room. She was wearing one of his T-shirts, hair still messy, looking like everything any man could ever want. "Ryan, I need to run, but if you can text me the reservation, that would be great."

"No problem, Mr. Holloway."

"Thanks, Ryan. You're the best." Grey ended the call and made his way over to Autumn. "I hope I wasn't talking too loud."

She squinted at him, seeming half-awake. "No, it's okay. I just really need my glasses."

Grey remembered that she'd taken them off when things were getting hot and heavy in the kitchen. He turned and grabbed them from the countertop and brought them to her.

She put them on and smiled. "So much better. Now you look like more than a blur with a spectacular head of hair."

Grey wrapped his arms around her waist and pulled her close. "I definitely do not want to be just a blur." He kissed her softly, trying to ignore the disappointment as it registered in his body. He'd thought they might be able to have the weekend together. That wasn't going to be the case.

"Did I hear you say something about a flight?"

He sighed and took her hand. "I have to go back to New York. Just for a few days." He then told her everything Ryan had said and explained the ramifications.

"Oh, wow. That doesn't sound good."

"It's pretty terrible." Grey couldn't help but notice that he would normally be seriously worked up about a situation like this. He always kept his cool, but that didn't mean he couldn't be a ball of stress on the inside.

"I'm so sorry."

"I'm the one who's sorry. I thought we could spend the rest of the weekend together."

Autumn painted on a smile, but Grey was fairly certain she was forcing it. However upbeat and endlessly sunny she could be, she wasn't great at faking it, or perhaps he'd learned to read her better. "It's okay. I have stuff to do around my house. Or I'll ask Molly if I can play third wheel with her and Mack."

Mack. That was something else he was going to have to deal with. His brother would *not* be happy about him leaving. Grey did not look forward to making that phone call. "I'm really sorry. Truly."

Autumn did that thing he often found her doing, where she dismissed something with a wave of her hand. "It's fine. I just need some coffee."

"Okay. Sure. Let me put on a pot."

Autumn walked around the kitchen island and acknowledged her dress and bra from the night before, which were draped over the back of a bar stool. "Oops."

"Yeah. I got up in the middle of the night to get a drink of water and found our clothes still on the floor." He poured coffee beans into the grinder, then filled up the carafe with water.

Autumn sat down, chin on one hand while watching him work. "I think you could get into breakfast if you just applied yourself. You're already a natural when it comes to coffee."

She was such a funny ray of sunshine. He felt horrible about the fact that he had to leave. "Maybe I could learn to appreciate it. With your help, of course." He brought her a cup of coffee, just like she liked it.

She blew on the hot beverage with pursed lips then took a small sip. "You made it perfectly."

"I pay attention." Grey's phone buzzed with a text—his flight information. "Looks like I need to leave for the airport in an hour or so."

"Okay."

"I'm just going to text Mack about it. He's probably still sleeping off last night." Grey tapped out as short an explanation as he could. He knew Mack would be disappointed, but hopefully he'd get over it.

"Let me drive you," Autumn said. "Then you won't need to deal with your rental."

"Okay. Sure. That would be great." He had a million things going through his mind, but he wanted to make sure Autumn was okay. "I just don't want you to think that I'm bailing on you. This thing at work is a real mess."

"Grey. I'm fine. I understand. I would do the exact same thing if I were in your shoes." She took another sip of her coffee then set down her mug and hopped up from the bar stool. "Come on. Let's get your stuff together."

"You really don't have to help."

She headed for the bedroom and looked back at him flirtatiously. "It will be faster this way. Then you'll have time for a shower. And I'll have time to get in there with you." She bounced her eyebrows at him.

"You are so smart." The woman was a genius. A very sexy genius. Why exactly was he considering getting on a plane in a few hours? Oh, right—like everything else in his life, he had yet another responsibility that was pulling him somewhere he didn't want to go.

# Eight

Autumn was determined to make the best of the fact that Grey was leaving. She was not going to dwell on the obvious in this situation—yet another man leaving her behind for New York. That was a silly way to think, she'd decided, even though that was precisely the first place her mind went when Grey told her what was going on.

But no, she wasn't going to let her history with her ex have that kind of power over her. In fact, she'd decided while they were watching fireworks, when the post-sex glow was still strong and before she had any idea that Grey would be leaving, that she would finally pack up the engagement ring and mail it back to Jared. That was her old life. The previous chapter. Sleeping with Grey meant that she had moved on. It wasn't like she was expecting a future with Grey. He didn't do serious and she'd known that from the very beginning. It was more that Grey had shown her that she was ready to be with a man, even if it was a summer fling.

"Is that everything?" Autumn asked when they'd packed the last of the items he'd pulled out of the bureau and closet.

"I guess? It's weird to pack when the place you're going to visit is home. Aside from what I brought here, everything I own is in New York. My whole life is there."

She didn't want another reminder of that sad truth. She didn't want to talk about details she found disappointing. Instead, she wanted more of Grey. Her fingers curled under the hem of his T-shirt, lifting it up over his head. She spread her hands across the smooth skin of his bare chest, biting down on her lip, "Time to get cleaned up."

He kissed her, possessively, like he wanted to leave his mark on her. "Yes, it is." He took her hand and led her into the bathroom. Glossy white marble tile, gleaming chrome fixtures and a large glass shower enclosure made for a luxurious and relaxing setting.

Grey turned the faucet handle, letting the water heat up while Autumn pulled off the T-shirt she was wearing, the one she'd stolen from his dresser. When he turned around, he unsubtly eyed her all the way down to her toes, his eyelids getting heavy, and the front of his pajama pants showing his true feelings on the subject of her, her body and the shower they were about to take. "You are way too beautiful."

He slid his hands around her waist and down to her bare bottom, squeezing. She rested her arms on his shoulders and kissed him, loving the hot and artful swirl of his tongue. The steamy bathroom air swirled around them. Water pattered against the glass. The shower was calling. Heat crept up Autumn's spine as she thought about Grey touching her, both of their bodies wet and slick. She reached to tug down his pajama pants, letting them fall to the floor.

Grey took her hand and stepped into the enclosure pulling her under the warm spray with him. He stood behind her, pressing his erection against her bottom. As the water warmed her body, he smoothed his hands down her hips and kissed her neck, curling the tips of his fingers into her skin but using a delicate touch with his mouth. The steam whirled around them and Autumn already felt drunk on his touch.

"Thank you for being so understanding about me leaving." His arms still threaded under hers, he rolled the bar of soap in his hands, making piles of creamy lather. Her nipples went hard with anticipation, then her breasts flooded with heat when he glazed the suds over her stomach and up to her breasts. She closed her eyes and soaked up every sensation. He held her breasts in his hands, plucked at her nipples with his fingers, sending sizzles of electricity between her legs.

"How could I not be when you're doing that?"

Laughing in her neck, he ducked one hand into the spray. Soap rinsed off, his hand skated down her stomach and dipped between her legs. His chest was pressed against her back, his length hard against her backside.

She wagged her hips back and forth as Grey groaned even more deeply than he had the night before. With his other hand, he took a single finger and drew delicate circles in the silky lather around her nipple, teasing her and drawing out the pleasure. The heat in the shower had reached its peak, but Autumn already felt like she was floating high above it all. As the pressure bore down on her hips, her reward felt so close, but she was dancing right on the brink. Teetering on the edge. Grey was solely focused on her pleasure. Round and round. Round and round. And then finally, the dam broke. Autumn's whole body froze, but Grey didn't stop, he only slowed down, using a gentler touch as he reacted to her gasps, coaxing one more wave of pleasure from her.

Feeling warm and content, she turned in his arms and delivered a deep kiss while she rode out the aftershocks reverberating through her body. All she could think about was leaving him happy. Leaving him satisfied. She sank down to her knees, dragged her hands down his hard abs, her fingers exploring the hard contours. She first took his length in her hand, then between her lips. Even that first touch had him groaning his appreciation. He gazed down at her through the steamy air, digging his fingers into her hair as the water cascaded down her back. The adoration on his face was mesmerizing, putting her into a near trance. On the outside, it seemed like he was carved out of stone, but Autumn knew now that what was behind those stern eyes was nothing short of pure passion.

His eyes drifted shut and she continued with her

charge, sucking in her cheeks to amp up the intensity. His mouth went slack. Every moan ended with a breathless gasp. He was on the verge. She could feel the tension. With one more deep groan, his hips froze in place and he came in quick pulses. Again and again. Autumn gripped his hips, and gently released him from her mouth, raising her face to the spray. Grey reached down and pulled her up by her armpits.

As she stood, they fell into a kiss that felt familiar now. Her brain was sending off warning flares—she was going too fast. She was allowing herself to fall and that wasn't a good idea. Her heart was telling her that a guy like Grey was everything she'd ever wanted or needed. Autumn had no choice but to intervene and remind herself that Grey was going to the airport. He had to leave. And she was going to have to do her best to not be sad about it.

Grey turned off the faucet and they stepped out onto the fluffy bath mat. They toweled each other off, kissing and smiling, happily caring for each other.

"I hate that I'm leaving." There was raw disappointment in his voice. Somehow that was of some comfort.

"Me too."

"But it shouldn't be long. A few days."

She took a deep breath and smiled, reminding herself that this might be for the best. As much as she was into the idea of spending time with Grey, she knew how inclined she was to go overboard. Her unwavering belief in love cut both ways—good *and* bad. His trip to New York would help her slow down. "Don't stay away too long. It's my birthday in less than a month and I don't want to celebrate alone."

"Why would you have to celebrate by yourself?"

Autumn shrugged, wondering if he felt put upon by the presumption that he would want to spend time with her on her birthday. They'd *just* slept together. It wasn't like they were dating. "Molly and I always go out on a girls' night, but I doubt she's going to want to do it this year. With the wedding and all, it doesn't seem likely. I don't have any family here, so that's out. Although I guess you could say that I don't have much family at all."

That struck Grey as incredibly sad. Right then and there, he made a resolution to make Autumn's birthday special. He wasn't quite sure what that would be, but there was time to sort that out. "Count me in."

"Really?" Autumn's voice bubbled with excitement.

"Yes, really." He kissed her on the end of her nose, but an abrupt noise made him turn his head in the direction of the great room.

*Boom. Boom. Boom.* Someone was pounding on the door to Grey's cottage. "Grey? I know you're still here. I can see your car."

"It's Mack," Grey said in a panic. He should've waited to text him. That was a stupid mistake.

Autumn was frantic, scurrying around the room, wrapped in a towel. "What do I do? My dress is hanging over the back of the bar stool in the kitchen. Which is totally visible from the windows on the back of the house. I have no clothes other than your T-shirt."

"Just stay here. I'll deal with him."

"Grey!" Mack knocked again. "I need to talk to you."

Thank goodness Grey had put the chain lock on the door. He wouldn't put it past Mack to use the keypad code and barge right in. He poked his head out of his bedroom doorway and shouted, "Two minutes. Hold tight." In a flurry, Grey dressed and rushed through the back door, purposely not letting Mack inside.

Mack was sitting on one of the patio chairs, legs crossed, bobbing his foot in agitation. He sprang from his seat as soon as Grey opened the door. "What the hell? You're leaving?"

Grey greatly disliked the tone of his brother's voice. "I told you last night that it was a possibility. Remember? At the party? I'm sorry I had to tell you by text, but I was in too much of a hurry to call." He would've been crazy to pass up that shower with Autumn in favor of a phone call with his brother.

"I understand that," Mack said. "What about your commitments here?"

"What about them? Pops is getting stronger every day. The renovation of the brewery is on track, Opal has more than enough work to do on the forensic accounting until I get back, and Autumn is doing a fantastic job."

"It's not about a to-do list. It's the principle of it." Mack blew out an exasperated breath, shaking his head. "You left my engagement party without saying goodbye. And speaking of Autumn, it's pretty obvious that she's in your cottage." With a nod, he gestured to her car, which was sitting next to Grey's rental. "Are you two sleeping together?"

Grey wasn't about to lie to his brother. "It just happened last night. It's casual."

"She just got her heart crushed, Grey. I hope you know to tread lightly. It would be cruel to break her heart."

"I understand. She and I had more than one conversation about it beforehand. Believe me, I will do anything to avoid getting mixed up in any of that."

Mack arched a skeptical brow at Grey. "Is that what you tell yourself? Because the easiest way to not get mixed up in something, is to *not* get mixed up in it. As in don't sleep with someone if you aren't willing to deal with the emotional fallout."

Was Grey being naive thinking that he and Autumn could keep things casual? He didn't think so. She seemed on board with all of it. She hadn't seemed fazed at all by his announcement that he was picking up and going to New York, and that had to be triggering for her. "I think you're underestimating her. And me, for that matter."

"Sorry. You're a grown man. I'm not going to tell you who you can have sex with. But can you please keep this quiet? We don't need the whole staff talking about it. And obviously, I would prefer it if there wasn't yet one more connection between our family and Autumn."

Grey had to stand there for a minute and process what Mack had said. "What are you saying?"

"That whole thing with her dad is a powder keg waiting to explode. And Autumn is an easy target. She's sweet and nice and unwittingly ends up the subject of pulpy articles all the time. It's just a matter of time before that all blows up in everyone's face."

Grey was overcome by a powerful urge to defend her. "I really don't appreciate your tone, Mack. Do you have any idea how hard she works to make weddings at Moonlight Ridge amazing? Because I've seen her in action, and let me tell you, she has a very particular skill set. One that is not easily replaced. We should be treating her like an asset to the resort. Not a liability."

Mack reared back his head. "Whoa. For the record, you don't sound like a guy who's embarking on something casual."

Grey took a deep breath. Mack was right. Grey was getting worked up. He needed to deescalate. "I'm tired of talking about this. I need to get back inside to grab my bag, so I can get to the airport."

Mack stepped closer. "We agreed to share the workload and I feel like you're shirking your responsibilities."

"It's only for a few days. My business is having an emergency. If anyone should appreciate the pressure I'm under, it's you."

"I also know that it's possible to get on a video call and fix most problems. You can do a lot remotely. That's what I've been doing and it works great."

Was Grey being irresponsible by leaving for New York? He really didn't think so. "Are you seriously asking me to not go?"

"It's your choice. But… I need you here."

Grey sucked in a deep breath and shoved his hands into his pockets. This argument he was having with

Mack was the perfect illustration of why he'd stayed away all these years. Why he'd let Mack and Travis live in their own orbits and he in his. There was always a problem. Controversy. And Grey despised it. This was how he'd been conditioned, from a very young age, the first time he saw his parents have a fight.

He turned and looked down at the lake. Guests were out walking and bicycling, enjoying the summer day. Part of him wished he could have their existence rather than his own. He hated feeling torn like this, but this was his life and he didn't have the ability to choose a different one. "I hate it when you do this."

"What?"

"Act so damn high and mighty. You are not a perfect person, Mack. However much you might think you are."

"I don't think that."

"Well, it can come off that way. The attitude that you know what's best for everyone is highly annoying. I can make my own choices, especially when it comes to my business. And my personal life."

"You still haven't told me if you're going or staying."

Grey turned back to the cottage and noticed Autumn's dress was no longer draped over the bar stool. She must've managed to grab it and sneak off without being seen. Grey wished he'd been around to witness that. He was certain it would've been adorable. If there was any bright spot in any of this mess, it was Autumn. If he stayed in Asheville, he would have more time with her, and he knew in his gut that he wanted that. Things had just started between them. The embers were still white hot.

"If it really means that much to you, I won't go."

"Seriously?" Mack seemed as shocked as Grey was by the answer.

"Yes. But I want you to cut it out with the guilt trip. I'm working my ass off here. Stop acting like I'm not pulling my weight."

"I will work on that. But I need you to start acting like you want to be here, rather than talking about it like it's nothing more than an obligation. I get it. I did the same thing. But you're with your family. And you're spending an entire summer in the mountains. Find a way to enjoy it. Most people would do anything to be in your shoes."

When his brother put it like that, it didn't take long for Grey to see that he'd been doing everything Mack accused him of. "You're right. You're absolutely right." Grey took another cleansing breath. "I'm really sorry that Autumn and I ducked out of your party. It was my idea. You can blame me for the whole thing."

"Eager to get somewhere?"

Grey had to fight his smile. "Yes. I think you're familiar with that scenario."

Mack nodded. "I am. I get it."

"I'm still sorry about it. And yes, I'll keep things with Autumn quiet. And don't worry, I will tread lightly."

"I guess this means Sunday lunch is on for tomorrow."

"I guess so. Pops will be happy."

"I'll let Giada know." Mack opened his arms wide. "Brotherly hug?"

Grey laughed. Perhaps that was Mack's real means of control—his charm was so disarming. "Of course."

Mack and Grey embraced for a moment, and Grey felt like he and his brother were back on track. He was glad he'd agreed to stay. For now.

They said their goodbyes and Grey rushed back inside. Autumn was waiting right inside the door with his suitcase, wearing the same jaw-dropping dress she'd been in last night. "Grey. I don't know when your flight is, but don't we need to get in the car?"

"Nope."

"Wait. What?"

"I'm not going. And the good news is that I'm definitely not going to miss your birthday." Grey could hardly believe that Mack had talked him into it, but he'd made a compelling case. "I'm not going. Mack laid a big guilt trip on me about fulfilling my obligations. He's right. I promised to stay for the summer. Taking off for New York would go against that."

"Do you think you'll be able to handle the problems you have at work?"

"I need to make a bunch of phone calls. Let people know the state of things. Then I'll address the whole company on Monday morning via video call. It should be okay. I will remind them that I'm away because my father has been ill. Hopefully that will put things in perspective."

"That's good. And I'm glad you're staying. Really glad." Autumn smiled warmly as a flush of pink colored her cheeks. Good God, she was beautiful.

"I'm glad, too." Grey wanted to sew up one more

thing, for both their sakes. He reached for Autumn's hand. "I need to ask you one more time, and I know that we've sort of beat this subject into the ground, but I need to know that you're really okay with this. With what happened last night. And an hour ago. And what might happen again later. If I'm lucky?"

Autumn slugged Grey on the arm. "Yes. I'm fine. Stop asking me about it."

He pulled her into his arms. "There's nothing wrong with having fun, right?"

"Never."

He kissed her softly. "Well, you, Autumn Kincaid, are all kinds of fun."

# Nine

It took Autumn more than two weeks to get around to packing up her old engagement ring. It wasn't that she hadn't been at home to do it. She definitely had, as Grey had stayed over multiple times since the Fourth of July. There had been dinners and a few movies on her couch, but more than anything, there had been sex. They were in the throes of that stage where you can't keep your hands off each other. Every time she was around him, she was burdened with questioning thoughts of when they would next get to be naked together. Things were that hot. And that good.

Autumn's cat, Milton, expressed some disdain at first, but seemed to be warming to her gentleman visitor. Yes, Autumn was plying the cat with extra treats, but she wanted the men in her life to get along. It was important. Grey was only there for the summer, and it was more than half-over. She wanted every minute to count and most important, to be enjoyable. She wanted zero drama. No problems.

Autumn planned to run to the post office at lunch after a morning of work at Moonlight Ridge. It was almost noon, so she pulled her purse and the small parcel out of her jumbo tote bag and set them on her desk.

Catering and Events manager Ross Barnes appeared in Autumn's doorway. "I have to run some errands at lunch. Need anything while I'm out?" He was always so helpful, and had a knack for showing up at exactly the right time.

"Any chance you'll be near the post office?"

"I'm actually meeting with a supplier nearby. What do you need?" He stepped into the room.

Autumn pointed at the package. "This needs to be mailed."

"Sure thing." He glanced down at the address label. "Jared? You're sending something to your ex?"

"I'm sending back my engagement ring."

"Why not just sell it? He dumped you with zero warning, days before your wedding day."

Ross had a point, but Autumn was trying to move on. "I don't need the money. Plus, it wouldn't feel right. I've already closed the door on that chapter of my life, but I'd like to flip the dead bolt, if you get what I mean."

He laughed. "I do. And I'm happy to help you do it. I take it you'd like it insured?"

"Yes, please. I also want someone to sign for it."

"No problem. My first job was in the mail room at

a law firm. I know all about that. I can take care of it and I'll bring you the tracking info when I get back."

"Thank you. I'll owe you one."

"Yep, you owe me big-time." Ross picked up the package. "By the way, did you see that Grey's friend moved out of her cottage today?"

Autumn really liked Ross a lot, but he loved to gossip, which was not Autumn's favorite activity. "I didn't. And she's a work colleague, by the way. Not his friend."

"What was she doing here? I don't think she ever really left the cottage. According to housekeeping, she never let them in. She took clean sheets and linens from them, but that was it. She only ever ordered room service. Doesn't that seem strange to you? It's the middle of the summer in the mountains of North Carolina. People pay a lot of money to come to Moonlight Ridge this time of year."

It did seem strange to Autumn, but Grey had been pretty quick to end the conversation when she'd asked about it before. "Everyone has their reasons for doing what they do. Maybe she needed alone time?"

He shrugged. "I guess."

Just then, Grey appeared in her doorway. Autumn hadn't come close to being immune to the effect of seeing him. Every glimpse made her happy. "I'm sorry. Am I interrupting something? I can come back." He had both arms behind his back and was clearly carrying something.

"No, Mr. Holloway. I was just leaving," Ross answered. "Autumn, I'll get this in the mail for you and bring you the tracking info later."

Grey stood to the side as Ross exited the room and disappeared down the hall. "Sending Ross to the post office? Don't we have on-site facilities for that?"

"It's personal. I'm actually sending back the engagement ring."

Grey's eyebrows arched inquisitively. "You didn't give it back at the time?"

Autumn shrugged. "It wasn't the first thing on my mind. I was too busy watching my life fall apart before my eyes. He never asked for it, either. But I don't like having it around. It needs to go." Autumn disliked this subject. She wished she would've sent the ring back earlier. Like the day after she got dumped. "What's in your hand?"

Grey then revealed what he was toting—a large handled basket. "Can I take you out to lunch?"

The heat started in Autumn's chest and raced straight to her face. "A picnic?" She got up from her desk.

"Yes. I guess Chef Hallie is testing some new lunch recipes and she wanted me to try them, but it's too nice a day to sit inside. So I asked the kitchen to pack us a picnic." He gazed down into her eyes. "Plus, I was thinking about that thing you said a few weeks ago. About how even when I'm busy, I should still have time to pop by your office. So here I am…"

Autumn grinned like a fool. "Popping by my office."

Grey planted a soft kiss on her lips. "Precisely."

Grey and Autumn walked downstairs and through the grand lobby, then outside. It truly was a glorious day for a picnic. The temperature was in the midseventies, there was very little humidity, and a pleasant breeze. "I was thinking we could go back to the garden behind the inn."

"Yes. Perfect. It's so pretty and quiet back there." They walked along the sidewalks that wound around the building, which led out onto the lush green space behind the building.

Grey spread out the lightweight blanket packed on top of the basket, and they both got settled. Autumn curled her legs off to the side and he sat on his knees while he pulled out the goodies Chef Hallie had prepared for them—a sandwich of French bread, prosciutto, fresh mozzarella and an oregano vinaigrette, along with several cold salads, one with farro and fresh dill, another with roasted corn and red pepper, and the last with seasonal fruit and mint. They also had a large bottle of sparkling water with lemon.

"I wasn't sure about wine on a Monday afternoon," Grey said, putting the empty containers back in the basket.

Autumn pitched in to help. "I'm already going to have a hard enough time staying awake this afternoon after all of that." Feeling quite full, Autumn stretched out on her side.

Grey put the basket aside and joined her, lying on his back and lacing his fingers together over his chest. "I thought it was quite good. Molly mentioned that sometimes there are complaints about the food."

"Hallie's trying her best." Autumn hadn't been able to see Grey the last few Sundays, as he'd been having lunch with his family and he hadn't extended the invitation. The one time she'd asked about it, Grey had said he'd rather save her from the drama, but Autumn had to wonder if it was something else. "Speaking of food, how was the family lunch?"

Grey shrugged. "Great. Giada's an amazing cook."

That hadn't quite been what Autumn was getting at. "Grey, I meant how was seeing your family?"

"It was fine. No big arguments, so that was good."

How he loved it when things were calm and even. "I heard that your work colleague moved out of her cottage today."

"More gossip going around?"

"It's just Ross. He knows everything that's going on. Plus, I think she naturally drew attention by not letting housekeeping in for an entire month."

Grey rolled onto his side and propped his head up with his hand. "Can you keep a secret?"

"Of course." Autumn couldn't imagine what he might say, but she was very good at holding them tight.

"First off, my colleague's name is Opal Terry. She was here because she was sorting out piles of old financial records for the business. My brothers and I discovered that things were in total disarray after Pops got sick. It's delicate work, in part because she's looking for discrepancies. We couldn't risk someone from housekeeping seeing what she was working on."

"Oh. Wow." Autumn was glad Grey had chosen to confide in her. It made her feel a little less bad about not warranting an invitation to Sunday lunch. "Do you think that someone on staff could be stealing?"

"We don't know enough yet. But that's why things were so cloak and dagger."

"Well, don't worry. I won't tell a soul."

Grey looked at his watch and sat up. "Dammit. I have to go. I'm supposed to meet Mack so we can talk about brewery stuff."

"I think it's wonderful that you're willing to jump through so many hoops to get Mack and Molly the wedding venue they want. And that you three brothers are going to such lengths to take care of your dad. It not only shows your love for him, I think it really shows your love for each other."

Grey dropped his head to one side and jutted out his lower lip. "How did you get to be so sweet?"

She leaned into him until her lips were an inch or two from his. "I think you know I'm not always sweet."

He grinned. "Do I get to see you later?"

Goose bumps rolled across her skin. "I'd love it."

"Perfect. I'll text you."

Grey strolled off, and Autumn stole her chance to admire him—the bold confidence of his stride, those sculpted shoulders she loved to touch, and that impossibly touchable head of hair. How was she going to feel when she had to watch him walk away for the last time? Would she be strong enough to simply focus on the countless assets of the man she'd been lucky to have? Or would it feel like she was losing someone who could have been more than a summer fling? She not only couldn't answer those questions, she didn't want to think about them. Not yet.

Lunch with Autumn had been amazing, and Grey was so glad he'd surprised her with it, but it had pointed out one glaring gap in his thinking about her. He hadn't been inviting her to Sunday lunches with his family because he didn't want to pull her too close. But he could see now that doing romantic things like bringing her a picnic could be just as hurtful—it was not the gesture of a casual relationship. This was a delicate balance, showing her how much he appreciated and adored her, without raising expectations that they might ever be more than friends and lovers.

Grey dropped off the picnic basket with the catering department and walked over to the barn. As he started up the hill where the building was situated, he marveled at the sheer number of trucks and vans on-site. Normally, the individual subcontractors do not like to work at the same time. Often, they *can't* work at the same time. You can't put in a floor when the plumbers are still running the lines that will go beneath it. But Grey and Jameson together had pulled some strings with Mountain Builders, all so they could make Mack and Molly's dream a reality.

When Grey arrived at the top of the hill, he could see that most of the workers had knocked off for lunch, sitting in the shade of a large red maple. This was the perfect time to discuss progress with Mack.

Grey grabbed a hard hat and walked inside. Mack was already waiting for him.

"You're here," Mack said. His voice was happy and upbeat, but also a bit raw.

"Of course." Grey hugged his brother, then placed his hand on his back. "Everything okay?"

Mack nodded. "Oh, sure. I just sort of had this moment where I realized this isn't like the other breweries. This isn't a normal opening. Molly and I are getting married in here. We used to run around as kids in this barn. It's just sort of crazy to think about."

It wasn't like Mack to be overly sentimental, but Grey completely understood what his brother was saying. "You're absolutely right. I think it only makes sense that the Moonlight Ridge location of Corkscrew Craft Beer Breweries be a special one. The wedding will make it even more so." Grey and Mack were both quiet for a moment, looking around the space. For Grey's part, he was thinking about the importance of getting everything right, but he also took a great deal of pride in the fact that he and his brother had embarked on this together. It felt good to be side by side.

"Does it look like we're on schedule?" Mack asked.

"Yep. It's going to be tight, but we should be all ready by that last weekend in August."

"It's like a month away." Mack drew in a breath so deep it made his shoulders rise a few inches.

"It's a little more than that. A month and two days. Don't worry. We'll make it." Grey was eager to change the subject. It seemed like it was doing nothing more than stressing out his brother. "So, Opal left today."

"I heard." Mack and Grey strolled back out through the barn door and took off their hard hats. "What was the upshot?"

"I haven't had a chance to fully absorb everything in her initial report, but I'd say there's quite a bit more money gone than we first thought. Maybe as much as a million."

Mack slowly shook his head in disbelief. "We're going to need to talk to a lawyer at some point, aren't we?"

"I'm thinking lawyers, plural. Somebody needs to go to jail if this all bears out. More importantly, this is going to take longer than we first thought."

"She couldn't find what she was looking for?"

Grey shook his head. "Let's just say she's frustrated. Every time she thinks she has an angle, evidence shows up and points her to a different department. Whoever is behind this is very clever with numbers so it's going to take longer than we hoped. But don't worry. She has photocopied everything and will work on it from home. There are still major pieces missing."

"Do we have a rough timeline?" Mack asked.

"It could take a few more months. Luckily, you now sign off on everything, so the money flow should stop."

Yet more concern clouded Mack's face. "I have to ask you a question, but I don't want you to freak out about it, okay?"

"You know I don't make a habit of that."

"Is there any chance that Autumn could be involved?"

"No. Absolutely not." Even Grey was surprised by the speed with which he gave his answer, but he was completely certain of this. "Autumn does not have access to billing or receivables. She hands everything off."

"Okay." Mack nodded.

"That's it? Just okay?" Grey needed to know if there was even a small chance that his brother was not convinced. "I know Autumn. She would never, ever do something like that."

"I believe you, Grey. You believed me when I said Molly had nothing to do with this. I'm trusting your instincts. Calm down."

Grey realized his heart was hammering away in his chest like a woodpecker on a sugar rush. "I am calm. I just want you to know that I know she would never do that."

Mack placed his hand on Grey's shoulder. "I don't think she would do it, either. I just had to ask. In part, because I felt like it was part of our due diligence. But also because I wanted to find out what's going on with you and Autumn."

"Nothing's going on. I mean, nothing beyond what you already know. We like spending time together."

"Sure. I know that. I also know that your car isn't at your cottage a lot of nights. And that you two had a picnic somewhere on the grounds today."

Grey narrowed his sights on Mack. "Are you spying on me?"

"No. But Molly and I are all over this property every day. It's not hard to figure out."

"We're just spending time together. There's no crime in that."

"I know. I'm just making sure you're cognizant of what you're doing. Or how deep you're getting. Because judging by the way you just defended her, you're in deeper than you think you are. I know that because I would absolutely defend Molly in the same way."

Grey dismissed the notion. "Autumn and I are fine.

We're just right. She's not as crushed by her broken engagement as you think she was. She sent her ring back to her ex today. Said she wanted to fully close the door on that part of her life."

"Do you think she's wondering if another door will open? Or maybe it already is open?"

Grey didn't see it that way at all. He saw it as a perfectly natural act for someone who was very good at accepting things and moving on. "No. I don't think so."

"Okay." Mack kicked at the ground with the toe of his shoe. "Do you ever wonder what would've happened if Pops hadn't had his brain episode?"

"Man, you are really being philosophical today, aren't you?"

"I've been thinking. So sue me."

Grey sucked in a deep breath. "Not really. I mean, I wished many times that it hadn't happened. Or that he could recover more quickly. But I didn't think about what life would have been like if it hadn't happened. In part, because I think life would've just gone on being the same."

Mack looked Grey straight in the eye. "Right. Which means that you and Travis and I wouldn't have been communicating with each other. We would've been on the same hamster wheel we've all been on for the last ten plus years."

Grey hadn't looked at the situation that way, and it knocked the breath right out of him. "Not really going anywhere."

"Maybe it's just the effect of Molly on me, but I'm trying to be better about looking at the bright side of things. As scary as it's been to see Pops struggle with his health, I do think some good has come out of this."

"Especially if we can get Travis back here."

"Yes. Absolutely. We need the time with Travis that you and I are having right now."

"I agree."

"Good. I'm glad. Because right now, I think you two are only set to overlap for my wedding. And that's just not enough time, especially considering that it'll be crazy busy."

"Are you asking me to stay beyond the end of the summer? Mack, we originally agreed to a couple of months each. Then when we discovered the financial problems we changed schedules again to stay longer. Next you asked me to skip a trip back to New York to fix a huge problem at my company. There's only so much I can do. I'm leaving Labor Day. Period."

# Ten

Autumn had never really liked her birthday that much when she was growing up. Well, that wasn't exactly true. She'd liked it before she was old enough to realize what was going on with her parents. Before that, her birthdays were magical events filled with balloons and fancy cupcakes, sparklers for candles and gifts far too expensive for a little girl. But once she turned twelve, she started to notice the venom between her mom and dad—the ways they would whisper terrible things to each other, argue, and eventually, ignore each other. Even after Autumn had gotten out of the house, her parents used her birthday to compete for her affection, trying to outdo each other with gifts. It was a sad, sad game.

The last few years in Asheville had been different.

She'd had simple birthdays out with Molly. They'd grab a cocktail somewhere, then go out for dinner or maybe go see live music. It was always fun and most important, easy. As she'd predicted, Molly felt a little too weighed down with everything she needed to do before the wedding. Instead of their usual routine they spent the afternoon getting mani-pedis and then had a quick lunch that ended with them splitting a huge piece of chocolate cake. Then her grandparents called from Australia, where they were spending the summer. They sang "Happy Birthday" to her and promised to see her soon. And the best was still yet to come.

Grey had invited her over so he could cook for her and they could have a quiet and romantic evening drinking wine out on his patio. It was going to be perfect. As soon as Autumn could decide on the right dress.

She'd tried on several different ones, trying to decide which one was right. She wanted to be sexy for Grey. Actually, she wanted his eyes to fall out of his head. Luckily, when she put on the last one she'd pulled out of her closet, she knew it was right. It was black with thin straps, a plunging neckline, and a bias cut that draped over her hips perfectly. Most important, the fabric was silky smooth against her skin, and she knew Grey would think it felt great under his hands.

She gave Milton an extra rub on top of his head, and was about to walk right out the door when a floral delivery person was marching up her front walk.

"Autumn Kincaid?" the man asked. He was carrying a lovely arrangement of all purple flowers—iris, tulips, salvia and coneflower.

"Yes. That's me." It seemed odd that Grey would send her flowers, especially since she was set to see him in a few minutes. But she took the vase and walked back inside with it. When she opened the gift card, her heart sank. The flowers were from her dad.

*Autumn, I know I haven't always been a good father, but I want you to know that I will always cherish you as my daughter. Happy birthday. With much love, Dad.*

To say she was torn would've been an understatement. Her mom had completely forgotten her birthday, which did happen from time to time. And it wasn't like her father had done anything directly to Autumn. But he'd done horrible things to her mom, to other women, and most important, he was the reason their family was in shambles.

She pushed the flowers to the center of her kitchen island and rushed out the door to go to Grey's. As soon as she was in the driver's seat, her grandmother's voice was in her head, telling her that she should never let a gift go unacknowledged. She wasn't prepared for a phone conversation with her dad, but she could send him a text.

The flowers are lovely. Thank you so much. She hit send, deciding that was plenty sentimental, but she hardly got her car started before he replied.

I'm on the Sunday Hour at the end of August. I hope you'll watch. You'll hear my side of the story.

Autumn couldn't imagine anything worse. Her dad on national television, telling his side? The thought turned her stomach sour. But that was weeks away, and tonight was supposed to be fun. She didn't reply to her dad. Instead, she drove straight to Grey's. When she walked around to the patio, she saw a setting that took her breath away. Grey had his back to her, lighting candles on the table, which was set with a crisp white tablecloth. His usual chairs weren't there, but instead there were lush upholstered ones Autumn recognized from the main inn. A bottle of wine was on ice. The fireflies were out. And Grey looked good enough to eat in dark trousers that made his butt look amazing and a light gray dress shirt with the sleeves rolled up to the elbows.

"Hey there," she said, coming up behind him and placing her hands on his shoulders.

He turned, all smiles, warming her from head to toe. Not even a heartbeat went by before he had his arms around her. "It's the birthday girl." He kissed her softly, then looked down at her, his eyes blazing. "How are you?"

"I'm great now that I'm here." She smoothed her hand over his chest, drawing in a deep breath. Her body was already on fire from just a single embrace. One kiss.

His hands roved up and down her hips. "Ooh. I like this fabric."

She laughed. He was not helping the fact that she didn't care about dinner. All she really wanted was him. "I thought you might like that."

"I love it. And I can't wait to take it off of you later."

He kissed her on the forehead. "But first, dinner. You sit and I'll be right back."

Autumn did as he asked, and a minute later, Grey brought out an artful salad with mixed greens, goat cheese, candied pecans and edible flowers. "It's so beautiful. And delicious."

"I'm more than just a pretty face," he joked, adding a wink before he took a sip of wine.

"So I'm gathering."

Grey got up to bus their plates, then disappeared inside. Autumn took her chance to enjoy the night. It was a bit warm for the mountains this late in the evening, but the breeze made it extremely pleasant. Grey returned with two similarly good-looking bowls of pasta. The aroma coming from the dish was incredibly appetizing.

"It's hand-cut fettuccine with wild local mushrooms, lemon zest and parmesan."

"You made pasta?"

He shook his head and took his seat next to her, refilling her wine. "I cheated. I bought pasta sheets at the store and cut them. Have a bite. It makes a huge difference."

She spooled the noodles on her fork and took a bite. It was a symphony of flavors, all perfectly balanced. "You are amazing. It's absolutely perfect."

"I wanted your birthday to be nice."

Autumn couldn't help it. Her eyes got watery. Her nose twitched. She wasn't going to cry, but it struck her as such a beautifully simple sentiment. "Thank you so much. It's better than nice. It's perfect."

Grey smiled, then dug into his pasta, and Autumn did the same. It didn't take long before they were both sitting back in their chairs, full and happy. "I have to say, I'm pretty proud of myself."

"You should be." She got up from her chair and collected his plate.

"Whoa. Wait. What are you doing? I'm supposed to wait on you."

"Come on. Let's go clean the kitchen. I need you to take off this dress."

"Yes, ma'am." He rushed inside behind her.

Autumn shouldn't have been surprised that Grey was the sort of guy who left the kitchen neat as a pin after cooking. "Where's the mess?"

He placed their bowls on the counter. "I clean as I cook. There's a sauté pan in the sink. And the bowls need to go in the dishwasher. Otherwise, it's all done."

"That sounds like things we can get to later." She grabbed his hand and led him to the bedroom. He didn't seem to need any more of an invitation.

She sat him down on the edge of the bed, standing between his knees. He looked up at her and drew in a deep breath through his nose, seeming to grapple with a few urges. Good. She'd been fighting a whole lot of her own. She reached down and unbuttoned two of his buttons, just to get a better view of his sexy chest. She couldn't wait to spread her hands all over his bare skin. She wanted to get lost in him.

His confident smile made an appearance—the one that said he was smart and he knew it. Sexy and he knew that, too. She wasn't going to begrudge him any of that. It was all so true.

He placed his palms on her hips, the heat from his hands nearly searing her skin through the dress. He curled his fingertips into her flesh and tugged her closer until her knees were flat against the side of the mattress. His face was close enough to her breasts that her nipples went hot and drew tight without a single touch. He trailed one hand to the center of her back and dragged the zipper drown. Electricity zipped along her spine as his fingers grazed her skin along the way. All the while, her need for him became more immediate. More impossible to tame.

One by one, she slipped the dress straps from her shoulders. The dress slid down the length of her body to the floor, turning up the heat another notch. Their gazes connected as she undid her strapless bra and wiggled her panties down her hips. Without a stitch of clothes, she was still wearing her heels. She put a foot on the bed and let him undo the strap. Then the other. All the while, Grey's eyelids were heavy with need, making her want to give him everything and anything he ever asked for. Autumn placed her hand on his shoulder and pushed him back on the bed, then planted her knee on the mattress between his legs.

"I like this side of you," he said. "The one that takes what she wants."

"It's very simple, Grey. I want you."

She removed her glasses and set them on the bedside table, then she leaned down and tugged his shirt out of the waistband of his pants. One by one, she undid the remaining buttons. The second his chest was bare, she stretched out alongside him and let her fingers roam, swishing her fingertips back and forth across his warm skin.

Grey rolled to his side and curled his hand around her nape, his fingers hot and needy. They kissed like they were both drowning and this was the only way to be saved. Their mouths were eager and open, ready and hot. Grey rolled her to her back, his thigh firmly rocking against her center, making heat flame between her legs. She'd never wanted him more. Maybe because she knew very well now what was in store.

He shifted to his knees and tore his shirt from his body, launching it across the room. She unbuckled his belt, then unhooked his pants and pulled down the zippers. She already felt the heat and tension radiating from his body. It was like the sun on an August day. He pushed his trousers past his hips, but that wasn't good enough for Autumn. She didn't want to wait. She sat up and tugged down his boxer briefs and took him in her hand, stroking lightly, letting her palm roll over the smooth skin of the tip with every pass. He groaned so deeply that the room nearly shook. Her other hand trailed down his taut stomach. She knew every carved contour, every incredible dip.

Grey hopped off the bed and got rid of the rest of his clothes, quickly climbing back onto the mattress. He pulled Autumn into his arms, kissing her intensely as their legs tangled. Their hands traveled everywhere—hers skimmed down his back to his magnificent backside, and his along the curve of her hip, then up to cup her breast. He rolled her to her back and their gazes connected as he drew delicate circles around her nipple. Blood and heat rushed through her body. Autumn felt like she might explode. It was as if he was touching her *hard* between her legs.

"Grey, please put on a condom. I want you. I need you."

He smiled and reached over to open the drawer and pull out a packet. He tore it open and rolled it over his length, never taking his eyes off her. Autumn felt both exposed and blissfully open. Needy *and* content. How did he do that to her? How did he put her in conflict with herself and make her happy to be there?

On his hands and knees, Grey hovered over her, then dipped his head lower. "What do you want for your birthday?" He huffed the question into her ear.

"I want you to set my world on fire."

As much as Grey wanted to look at Autumn, his eyes clamped shut as he sank down into her. The warmth and gentle pull of her body was familiar and had been in reach all this time, but tonight it felt as if he'd gone without her forever. The sensation made a sharp breath leave his chest, made his abs pull tight, but then air filled his lungs and he felt the tension give ever so slightly. Just enough to let him enjoy every second of being with Autumn.

He lowered himself, planting both elbows on the bed. He kissed her full, sexy mouth. The one full of sweetness and clever words and laughter. The one that gave him pleasure he could get lost in forever. She wrapped her legs around him, caressing the backs of his thighs with her ankles. Up and down, like a rolling wave, tugging him out into a deeper and deeper bliss.

Autumn tilted her hips, allowing him to plunge deeper inside her. He skimmed his mouth over the velvety skin of her cheek, along the curve of her jaw and down the delicate slope of her neck. They moved together in a rhythm that worked so well for them both. Grey could tell from her breaths, which were shallow and restless, and the roll of her hips, which was more insistent now. Grey was intent on giving her everything she wanted, so he pushed up from the bed, sucking in his abs, trying to stem the coming tide of his own orgasm as he took his thrusts longer and more intense. His thighs felt like they were on fire, the pressure relentless on his hips, tightening in his groin. He listened to Autumn, studied her face for clues as she dug her fingers into his back, holding on to him for dear life. She turned her head to the side, and he lowered his head, kissing her neck and drinking in her smell. She arched into him, humming her approval, muscling him closer with her heels.

He could tell she was close. He felt the tightening inside her. He remained focused on her, trying to ignore the intensity of how good every inch of her felt. His mind was blurry at the edges, a soft fog rolling into his consciousness. Her mouth went slack, her breaths halting and almost musical. She dug her fingers in deeper and reined him in even closer with her legs. And then she unraveled, arching her back and gasping. It was so stunning to watch that he hadn't noticed how close his own climax was, and it slammed into him like a line drive from out of nowhere. He sank all the way down into her one more time and dropped his head, planting his face right into the glorious valley of her neck.

Autumn hummed and rolled them to their sides, where they could kiss and float back to earth in the comfort of each other's arms. There was a part of his mind that would be blank for a while, but there were several thoughts winding their way through his brain. All he could think about was the complete switch between the way he'd felt when he'd come back to Asheville at the beginning of the summer and the way he felt now. He'd thought he'd spend the time just waiting to leave. Now, there were formerly improbable ideas in his head.

"Mmm. You are amazing, Grey Holloway." Autumn trailed her fingers up and down his side, waking up his body all over again.

"Happy birthday, Autumn. I hope it was a good one." He was so glad they'd had the chance to share this together. It would be a memory he'd hold on to for a long time. Quite possibly forever.

"It was the best. The absolute best."

"It's not over yet. There's dessert."

Autumn reared back her head. "Ooh. What kind?"

"Yellow cake with chocolate buttercream. A real birthday cake."

"Did you make it for me? Are you seriously that talented?"

The idea was ridiculous, but he loved that she saw it as possible. "I had the pastry chef make it for you."

"You are so sweet. I don't even know what to do with you." She kissed him softly.

"Do you want some now?"

"Actually, I was thinking about something while we were sitting outside and having dinner. It's such a warm night and the pond is so nice this time of year."

"You want to go swimming?"

"What about skinny-dipping?"

For a moment, Grey wondered what in the hell she was thinking. "We can't do that. This is my family's property."

"No one will see. The guests only know about the main lake, not the pond at the back of the property. Molly took me there once."

As kids Grey and his brothers swam in that pond every day. Sometimes Molly joined them. They considered it their private swimming hole. One summer they even built a tree house overlooking the pond. But that was years ago...

"How do you know for sure the guests don't use it now?"

"Okay. Fine. I don't know that for sure, but we're both smart people. We can figure out a way to make it happen if we apply ourselves."

"I don't know..." This was not something Grey wanted to do. Except that he did very much enjoy being naked with Autumn. And he did want to make her happy.

"Oh, come on. When was the last time you did it? I bet it's been a while."

"Never. I've never done it."

Autumn gasped. "Then we have to. No excuses." She hopped up from the bed and grabbed her dress, stepping into it and threading her arms through the straps. "Come on. Throw on a T-shirt and a pair of shorts."

Grey did as Autumn had asked, fishing the garments out of his dresser and putting them on. "This is insane."

"Just think how ready you'll be for cake after this." She turned her back to him. "Just zip it up part of the way. So I can get out of it quickly."

"After this, I'll be ready to get you back in my bed."

Autumn laughed. "Swimming first, then cake, then sex."

"Yes, ma'am." They walked out into the living room. "Do we take towels?"

"Probably too obvious while we're walking down there. We do need to scout it out to make sure the coast is clear. Also, you're going to have to do that part because I have to leave behind my glasses."

*Oh, right.* Grey realized that he and Autumn were going to have to guide each other through this scenario. "What do we do if we get down to the water and there are a bunch of people down there?"

"Wait until they leave. But you're so far back on the property, I doubt we'll see anyone and they won't see us, either." She kissed him, and it felt like a wish for good luck. "Come on."

Hand in hand and barefoot, they walked outside and Grey closed the door behind them, thankful the cottage had a keypad entry and he didn't need to worry about losing a key. Through the dark of night, they fast-walked along the overgrown pathway to the pond. They gained speed as they got closer. The air was right on the edge of warm and cool, making the senses come alive. The grass was soft against the soles of Grey's feet. Autumn's hand fit perfectly in his. Everything smelled sweet, and the bullfrogs and crickets were taking turns being loudest.

There was no one in sight when they arrived near the water's edge, standing under cover of a large tree. "Ready?" Autumn asked. She didn't wait for an answer though, wriggling out of her dress.

Grey sucked in a breath and stole a moment to look at the sumptuous curves of her body, lit up by the moon. "Yeah. Okay." He shucked his shorts and lifted his T-shirt over his head, then collected their clothes and left them in a bundle at the base of the tree trunk.

Autumn took his hand again. "You have to go first. I'll either jump too soon or fall right into the water."

Grey's heart was thumping wildly, but something about being with Autumn made him willing to throw caution to the wind. "Okay. Follow me." He decided a quick approach was the best, taking six or seven long hurried strides and leaping into the water. It was warmer than he imagined. His head went right under. And Autumn's hand slipped from his. Grey kicked hard to get back to the surface, shaking his head. "Autumn? Where are you?" He felt frantic, squinting into the dark, and treading water to stay afloat.

Then he heard the surface break and a deep breath. "Wow. The water feels amazing." Autumn was just fine. She'd only swam a little farther than he would've liked. "Grey?"

Now he could see her outline against the blue and black ripples of water. "On my way." He swam over to her and immediately pulled her into his arms. Their legs tangled as they both kicked to stay afloat.

"So?" she asked. "Fun?"

Yes, the experience itself was nothing short of enjoyable. But he knew that it wouldn't be the same without her. But he didn't know how to say that to her. He was supposed to be treading lightly. This was just for the summer. Nothing else. "The best."

She broke free from him and swam a few strokes away, then turned and came back.

"What are you thinking about?" he asked.

"How you're too handsome for your own good." She kissed him, soft and wet and breathless.

He laughed and kissed her back. "That's sweet, but I know you're blind without your glasses."

"That's where I've got you. I'll always remember exactly what you look like."

# Eleven

This was Jameson's favorite activity—watching Giada cook in his kitchen for Sunday lunches with his boys. They'd managed eight Sundays since the engagement party. Now it was only a week until Mack and Molly would be married, and Travis was coming home for a few months. All would be right with Jameson's world. Well, as long as he could convince all three of his sons to stay in Asheville permanently. For now, the most pressing matter was Grey. Time was dwindling, but he and Mack had a plan.

"Are you sure I can't help?" Jameson walked up behind Giada as she whisked up a homemade vinaigrette for the salad. He placed his hand on the small of her back and leaned down to kiss her neck.

Giada turned and shot him a look. "Your sons will

be here soon. And yes, you can help. You can put the greens in the salad bowl."

Jameson loved both sides of Giada—the taskmaster and the caring nurturer. Fire and ice. She was everything he wanted in a woman. If only he could convince her that it was a good idea. "Got it." He did as she asked, glad that this was now as simple a task for him as it would be for anyone else. He was getting better. He felt alive, especially when he was with Giada.

She opened the oven to check on a large baking dish of her signature recipe, which Jameson had dubbed eggplant Giada. It was a classic Greek moussaka with a few Italian twists like fresh basil. She put both love and her heritage into everything she cooked. "Another ten minutes. Then it needs to cool."

"All done with the salad. What now?"

"We need to talk about your new habit of touching my hip and kissing my neck, *cara mio*. It's not good to have that happen in front of Grey and Mack."

"Why?" He and Giada had kissed several times since the night of Mack and Molly's engagement party, but it wasn't nearly enough for Jameson. He wanted more and he'd been quite plain about it. "They adore you and they want me to be happy."

"They also pay my salary. I'm supposed to be taking care of you. I'm not supposed to be in your bed."

"But you aren't in my bed. I've extended the invitation and you've declined."

She smiled and stepped closer to him, taking his hand. "I care for you, Jameson. I think you know that. But your health is more important than romance. The doctor wants you to focus on healing and I agree. I know your boys do, too."

"But I feel fantastic. I feel perfect, really. I'm hardly using the cane at all. We're walking farther every day, and that's even in this crazy heat wave we've been having." Speaking of crazy heat, Jameson felt like his entire body was on fire every time he got her to talk about something of consequence. All too often, she blew off any conversation about the two of them having a relationship outside of nurse and patient.

"You're doing really well. I'm proud of how hard you've worked. But I still worry."

"Maybe that's because you care." He rubbed the back of her hand with his thumb, peering down into her lovely face. Her dark hair was pulled back, showing the silvery strands that brought out the aquamarine of her eyes. Her lips were full and beckoning.

"Jameson…" she said as he lowered his head.

"Shhh." Jameson gently threaded his hand into her hair, carefully placing his lips on hers. The instant they met, he was reminded how badly he wanted her. Giada's hand went to his waist, subtly tugging him closer. Jameson followed her cues, wrapping one arm around her. His heart began to beat fiercely. His thoughts swirled. His feet felt unsteady. And then he faltered, lurching to the side. He caught himself on the countertop with one hand.

"Are you okay?" Giada asked in a panic.

*Dammit.* "I'm fine. Perfectly fine." He straightened, still feeling dizzy, but unwilling to admit that to her.

"This is what I'm talking about. You are not ready for this, Jameson, however good you might be feeling."

"It's just my body reminding me how badly I want you. It's not my health. It's my heart."

The kitchen timer buzzed. Giada checked the oven just as the doorbell rang. Mack's voice called from the front hall. "We're here." He and Molly strolled into the kitchen with a bottle of wine and a large arrangement of colorful summer wildflowers. Thank goodness his son was still announcing himself. Two minutes earlier and Jameson and Giada would've been found kissing like a couple of teenagers.

"These are for Giada," Molly said as Jameson kissed her on the cheek.

Giada removed the oven mitts and accepted the bouquet. "*Grazie*. It's very kind of you. Although, it seems to me like the bride-to-be should be getting the flowers around here. Not me."

"Hard to believe, huh? A week until we get married." Mack took a seat at the kitchen island.

Molly stood next to him. "Actually, it's only six days. By this time next week, we'll be married."

Giada was busy filling a vase at the sink with water. She brought it to the island and began artfully arranging the flowers. "When will Travis arrive?"

"Not until Friday. He's so ridiculously busy," Mack said, folding his arms across his chest. "But at least he'll be here."

"And when is Grey set to leave?" Giada asked.

"Labor Day." Jameson looked over at Mack. "Any thoughts on how we bring this up?"

Giada shook her head. "Jameson, Grey is a grown man. If you want him to stay, just tell him you want him to stay."

"Grey needs a nudge," Mack said. "He'll do anything to avoid upheaval and drama. It's too easy for him to stay in New York and live a quiet life he controls."

Mack was not wrong about Grey, but Mack also didn't fully understand the home Grey had come from. Both boys had been so young when they'd come to live with Jameson. "True, but you have to appreciate why he is drawn to stability and quiet. His parents were anything but that. A child grows up in chaos, especially when they're an only child, and they'll do anything to avoid it. That doesn't go away."

Quiet fell upon the room, but then Molly spoke up, "I get that. My entire family is a mess. But maybe we just need to remind Grey that the one he has here is ultimately supportive and loving."

Jameson felt a certain degree of pride that Molly saw his family that way, but he also knew the truth. His sons had not fully healed the wounds of the past. And none of that could really happen until Travis was in Asheville as well and they had time to work things through. Which meant they had to convince Grey to stay, at least for a little while longer. "He's bringing Autumn for the first time today. That's got to be a good sign for our case."

Mack shrugged. "Maybe. Don't you think it's strange he waited this long? They're spending so much time together. I just think he's sending a lot of signals about leaving soon."

"Don't be so negative," Molly said. "You don't know what's going to happen. Maybe it will just take the right woman. Autumn might be that person."

Mack reined Molly into a hug. "Do you want to know what I love about you?" He kissed her on the top of her head. "You aren't afraid to tell me to stop being a jerk."

They all laughed, but Jameson's faded quickly. He had so much to be thankful for in his life, but he also had an awful lot weighing on him—Giada, Grey and the hope that his sons would reconcile.

Grey and Autumn heard laughter as they approached his Pops's house. He was about to walk right in, when Autumn stopped him with a hand on his arm.

"Hold on a sec," she said. "I just want to say thank you for bringing me. It means a lot."

Grey was torn. He didn't want it to mean too much. There was a reason this was the first time he'd invited her to a Sunday gathering—it would be just another way in which they'd become too close. He'd only relented because Pops had given him a hard time about it. "I'm sorry. I should have invited you before. I guess I wanted to shield you from my family's drama."

Autumn cast him a dismissive look. "Grey. You want drama, you get my family. Your family is wonderful. I'm so relieved I get to be here while my dad is doing his interview this afternoon on *The Sunday Hour*. I can avoid the whole thing."

Grey glanced at his watch. *The Sunday Hour* was already starting, and the interview with Autumn's father would begin any minute. "You're not worried about that?"

She painted a smile on her face, but it was that same expression she had when things got stressful at work and she felt like she had to power through it. "A little, but I'll be fine." Autumn nodded at the door. "Let's go in."

Grey opened it for Autumn, then followed her inside. There was still laughter and talking coming from the kitchen, all the sounds of a happy household. Grey did have a great deal of wonderful memories of this house, and now that he'd been back in Asheville for a few months, it no longer felt like stepping back in time to be here. When they walked into the kitchen, they were greeted warmly by Giada, Pops, Mack and Molly, with hugs all around. Even the dogs got in on the attention, their tails wagging as everyone petted them.

"Thank you for joining us, Autumn," Pops said.

"Thank you for including me. It feels like a real honor," Autumn answered.

Grey again felt like such a jerk. Why hadn't he included her earlier? Autumn didn't really care about family drama. And if anyone could make an uncomfortable situation better, it was her. "Lunch smells amazing, Giada."

"Thank you, Grey. Everything is ready. We should sit down and eat."

Grey and Mack helped bring dishes to the table as everyone got settled in their seats. Pops was at the head of the table, just as he'd always been, every bit the proud patriarch. He began passing food, and Grey had to admit that his dad was looking healthier and stronger every day. The difference between now and when he'd first come home was like night and day.

"So, I have kind of a funny story," Molly said as everyone ate. "Two of our guests were taking a moonlight hike around the property and saw people skinny-dipping in the pond. A man and woman. It was too dark to get any details or identification. I wonder who they saw?"

Grey choked back a snicker as Autumn elbowed him in the ribs. "Wow. That *is* funny," Grey said.

"Good thing we haven't started renting out the renovated tree house yet," Mack said, smiling. "Although I suppose this is an argument for putting in more security cameras, eh, Grey?"

Dammit! Mack knew it was them.

"My sons love to spend my money," Pops said, thankfully oblivious.

"That's not true. Do you know that the brewery is going to be entirely self-sufficient for electricity? Between the solar panels on the roof and the other energy-efficient measures. It's going to be amazing. And a big money saver."

Jameson looked down the table at Grey. "Really, son?"

Grey didn't entirely understand the question. "Well, yeah, Pops. That's what I do. Green architecture."

"I know that," Jameson said, waving him off and wiping the corner of his mouth with a napkin. "I guess I didn't realize that it could make that big of an impact."

"The technology moves so fast. It's pretty amazing what can be accomplished."

"I've been wanting to talk to you about all of that, Grey," Mack said, putting down his fork and taking a sip of wine.

"What, exactly?" Grey asked.

"I'd really like to go back and update all twenty-five Corkscrew Craft Beer Brewery locations with solar and wind power. Water reclamation. The whole nine yards."

"There are consultants who can help you with that. I can connect you with a few people," Grey offered.

"That's not what I want. It's like when I asked you to do the design for the brewery at Moonlight Ridge. I want to work with you. Partner for real."

"Oh." Grey was a bit taken aback. "That's not really what I do, but I'm sure we could work something out. You know I'll help you with anything you need."

"I think you know what I'm asking, Grey. And I feel like you're avoiding the question." Mack shook his head.

"Just say it, Mack." Grey looked around the table, hoping someone would see that his brother was making things uncomfortable. Autumn shifted in her seat. Molly downed the last of her wine.

"I want you to move to Asheville permanently and work with me."

Autumn sharply sucked in a breath then nearly lunged for her water. The ice rattled in the glass.

"We've talked about this, Mack. I'm not going to throw away more than a decade of work by leaving behind my business in New York."

"You don't have to throw it away. Just hire someone to run that office. Or heck, see if some of your people want to move out here. It's a lot cheaper to live in North Carolina."

"And it's so pretty in Asheville," Molly added. "People with families appreciate that."

"If anyone can tell you it's the perfect place to raise kids, it's me," Pops said.

Grey could see this for what it was—an ambush. "Pops, you're in on this, too?"

The guilty look that fell across Dad's face was all Grey needed to see. "I'd rather have you here. That should have always been obvious. I love you, Grey. Your brother loves you."

Grey felt like there was a tug-of-war going on and he was the rope. He was being pulled between his old life and the new. He glanced over at Autumn, knowing she was a big part of this equation. He cared for her deeply. He wanted to see her after he went back to New York. But he also knew that she was looking for a lifetime of love—real commitment. Grey wasn't there yet. She'd been the first woman to ever question his beliefs about love, but it wasn't like decades of thinking one thing could disappear in a few weeks. He was someone who thrived on certainty and stability. Love could guarantee neither.

"Tell me you'll think about it," Mack said. "An answer before the wedding would be great. Especially since you're scheduled to go back soon."

That really irked Grey. He felt like he'd already answered this question. The fact that Mack was asking it again so soon before a momentous event in Mack's life only made the guilt that much worse. What was Grey supposed to do? Go to his brother the day before his wedding and turn down his offer? Grey would never live it down. Mack said he wanted to heal the fissures between the brothers. It was times like this that Grey questioned whether that was really true.

Autumn loved the way the Holloway family made her feel at home. Except now, the spat between Grey and Mack had made everyone uncomfortable. Autumn tried to hold on to her smile, but on the inside, she was crumbling. This was the one thing that had been dogging her for weeks—Grey was leaving. It was about to be over. And the fact that even his brother couldn't convince him to stay, made it even worse.

"I think we should change the subject," Molly said, winking at Autumn. Thank God for her best friend. She understood how much the affection between Autumn and Grey had grown all summer, and that had left Autumn feeling exceptionally vulnerable. Again.

"Wonderful idea," Giada said. "Autumn, tell me about your family. I don't know anything about them."

Autumn was ready to run out of the room. It was like all of the previous awkwardness had grown exponentially. "I'm an only child. My parents are divorced. My dad lives in Los Angeles, but he's always traveling. My mom goes back and forth between Santa Barbara and Miami."

"Oh, I see." Giada smiled. "And what does your dad do that he travels so much?"

Now Autumn simply wanted to throw up. A headache was brewing. She'd told herself she could ignore her dad's interview, but now she was confronted with the subject of him anyway. "He works in film."

Molly reached for Giada's hand, which was on the table. "Giada, this is a difficult subject for Autumn. Something tells me that you don't know who her father is."

Giada looked around the table, surprised. "I'm sorry. I don't."

Molly looked to Autumn, silently asking for approval to explain. Autumn nodded, but didn't say a thing.

"He's a very well-known Hollywood producer," Molly said. "He's also been in the news quite a lot because women have made allegations of sexual harassment."

Autumn swallowed hard, willing the tears to stay away. She forced herself to smile, but it felt so fake it was torture. "That's pretty much it. My mom is erratic and not much of a mother, to be honest, but she also had a toxic marriage, so it's hard to blame her." Autumn felt like she was shrinking into nothingness. The deep sense of shame she felt for something she'd played no role in was difficult to bear. Most of the time she did a good job ignoring it. But at times like this, when it was unavoidable, it all came crashing down on her.

Grey put his hand on her back. "You okay? Do you want to step outside and get some air?"

Now Autumn wanted to cry twice as hard. Grey was so sweet and kind. He understood. He was also leaving in a week, and he'd just demonstrated during the argument with Mack that he was dedicated to doing exactly that. Why did everything have to be so terrible? "Yes, please. Excuse us for a minute." Autumn put her napkin on the table and Grey pulled her chair back for her.

Giada rose from her seat and scrambled over to them. "*Cara mia*, I feel terrible. I had no idea. I don't know anything about Hollywood. I read romance novels and watch British mysteries on television. I'm as out of the loop as they come."

Autumn shook her head, not wanting Giada to feel bad. It wasn't her fault. She was showing an interest in Autumn. She'd been welcoming. "It's okay. Truly. You had no idea." She turned to Grey who had just as much pity on his face as everyone else at that table. "I just need a minute outside."

Grey took Autumn's hand and led her out through the patio doors to the backyard. Merely stepping outside felt like permission to fall apart, especially when she flashed back to the last time she'd been out here— Mack and Molly's engagement party. She and Grey had so much fun that night, flirting and dancing, and starting to fall under each other's spell.

Grey didn't say a thing. He just had that compassionate look on his face, the one that said he didn't know what to do to make the situation any better, which was frustrating, because he had the power to make so much of what she was feeling go away.

Her phone buzzed in her pocket, but she ignored it. "I'm a lot of fun at parties," she said, hoping to lighten the mood.

Grey pulled her into his arms and kissed the top of

her head. "You're the most fun. Everyone else needs to take fun lessons from you."

She peered up at his handsome face. She wished so badly that he wouldn't leave. Thinking about it caused a burning pit in the middle of her stomach. But she also didn't want him to have to be talked into it. She wanted him to decide on his own that Asheville was for him. She wanted him to conclude on his own that *she* was for him. Because the truth was that she had fallen so hard she didn't know how she was going to survive his leaving. There would be no quick bounce back this time. Her phone buzzed again. Then again. "My phone is blowing up."

"Frantic bride?"

It buzzed again. "On a Sunday afternoon?"

One more buzz and Autumn had to look. She fished it out of her pocket, only to see a long string of texts from her old friends in LA.

I can't believe he used you as a shield.

I'm so sorry your dad dragged you into this.

What a jerk! Just because you still love your dad doesn't mean he isn't terrible.

Autumn felt her hand go so cold she nearly dropped her phone.

"What is it?" Grey asked.

She showed Grey the messages, not knowing exactly

what any of this meant, but certain it had something to do with her father's appearance on national TV.

"The interview?" Grey asked.

"It must be."

He pulled out his own phone and in less than a minute, he had a video clip. "I think I found it." He pushed play, and there she saw her dad, looking unwell. He'd lost at least twenty pounds. His face was gaunt. His skin was ashen, his eyes drawn. Still, she couldn't help it. She saw that face and she still saw her dad. He hadn't been perfect to her, and he hadn't always been there, but she still loved him, even if she hated the things he'd done.

"What's your biggest regret?" the interviewer asked.

"That my daughter Autumn got stuck in the middle of this. She's such a lovely person. I'd like to show you the text she sent me on her birthday. It meant the world to me."

He handed his phone to the interviewer, then the text was displayed on the screen. The flowers are lovely. Thank you so much. I hope you know I love you. You're the best dad a girl could ever have.

"That's not what I said," Autumn blurted. "Half of that text is fake."

"Hold on. Let's listen," Grey said.

"Some people might wonder how a man who has such a close relationship with his daughter could turn around and harass women," the interviewer said.

"Maybe you need to ask a different question," her dad said. "Would a man who adores his daughter ever treat women badly? The answer is no."

Autumn felt absolutely sick to her stomach.

Grey put his phone inside his pocket. "We need to hire a publicist. Make sure someone knows that you didn't say those things. Do you still have the original text on your phone?"

"I do, but you know what's going to happen. People will want to hear my side of the story. And then it's just more negative publicity because someone who works for my dad will start poking holes in it. Or they'll say that I'm an ungrateful daughter. It will never end."

"Shh. It's okay." Grey again pulled her back into the comfort of his warm embrace. "It might be hell for the next few days, but it'll be gone in a week."

Autumn froze. A rousing round of laughter came from inside the house. Yes, she felt horrible about the situation with her dad. But the real reason this was getting to her was because Grey was leaving. She lifted her head from his shoulder and looked up into his face. "You'll be gone in a week, too, Grey. So it won't even matter, will it?"

He rolled his neck and let go of her, then looked up at the sky, seeming exasperated. "Are you going to lay into me just like my family?"

She shook her head, fighting back the tears. She didn't cry often. She'd always put so much stock in being upbeat. But sunny Autumn was gone right now. She was too damn sad. She loved Grey and she'd been too afraid to say it. To anyone, even herself. What they had was supposed to be a fling. It hadn't turned out that way. Not in her heart, at least. "I'm not going to lay into you. It's your choice, Grey. It's always been your choice to stay or go."

"Do you not understand how frustrating this is? As far as I'm concerned, it was never a question. I told everyone from the outset that I was going to go back to New York. Everyone knew that all along and everyone's acting now like I'm the jerk for sticking to what I always said I would do."

"I can see your point. I also just sat there and watched your family plead with you to stay. They love you, Grey. Do you not see how lucky you are? Do you know how much I wish I could have what you have?"

"They're not perfect, Autumn."

"Of course they aren't. No family is. But if there's love there, the rest isn't important. At the end of the day, love is all that matters."

He grumbled and looked down at the ground. "We aren't talking about my problems right now, anyway. We're talking about yours."

She reached for his arm, and she felt in that one touch that he was already leaving. He was going to follow through on everything he promised—going back to New York. Keeping things fun. Except nothing felt fun right now. "Grey. My problem *is* your problem. Do you have any idea how hard it was to sit there and listen to Mack and your dad make their case and for me to hear you dig in your heels?"

Grey looked down at her, with the darkest look she'd ever seen in his eyes. "You knew I was leaving, Autumn. Just like everyone else. This was not a surprise."

She drew in a deep breath through her nose. "You're

right. It wasn't a surprise. The surprise was how sad it made me. The surprise was how much I feel like the whole world is falling out from under me right now."

"Of course you feel like that. The stuff with your dad is terrible."

She shook her head so fast her hair whipped. Overhead, there was a rumble of thunder. The wind had picked up. "It's not that. I feel like I'm falling apart because of you. The thought of you leaving is killing me and I've been convincing myself that I was fine with it. Well, I'm not fine, Grey. I'm not fine with you leaving." She sucked in one more breath for courage. The words were right there on her lips, waiting to come out, and she realized she'd been holding them for days. Weeks. "I don't want you to leave because I love you."

Raw disappointment crossed his face. "Autumn…"

"I know. I know. I told you that I was fine with the idea of just having fun, and I was." She looked back at their summer and realized that wasn't entirely true. "Up until a point. But my feelings started to change. And I didn't want to go back on everything I'd said to you."

"I don't think you know what you're saying right now. You've just had all of this upheaval because of your dad, and you're feeling emotional. This isn't a good time to talk about this."

A raindrop landed on the end of Autumn's nose. She looked up and another hit her forehead.

"And see? It's starting to rain. Let's get inside," Grey said.

Autumn stood firm. "No. I don't want to go inside. I want to stand out here and get soaked. I want to talk about this. Because I've spent my entire summer not talking. Not telling you the depths of what I was feeling for you."

Grey looked back and forth between Autumn and the patio door. "I don't know what you want me to say. I don't believe in the same things you do. You knew that about me from very early on."

"I don't believe you don't feel something for me."

"Of course I feel something for you. But whatever it is, I don't think it's that."

Autumn had her answer. "You don't love me."

His shoulders slumped. "I don't know. I don't know what you want me to say."

Autumn pressed her lips so hard together that it hurt, but she had to do something to stem the tide of pain that was welling up inside of her. "Maybe you should just say goodbye."

"We have six more days together. Why would I do that?"

"Six days or six minutes. Waiting is just going to make the final goodbye that much harder. If you're really going, I'd rather say it now."

"What does that mean?"

"It means goodbye."

# Twelve

Autumn had to drag herself out of bed on Monday morning. She was running on no sleep and a broken heart—not a good way to start the week. She'd stupidly held out hope that Grey might change his mind about leaving. Now she knew that nothing could keep him here. Not even her.

There had been thunderstorms all night long, the rain beating against the windowpanes as Autumn was curled up into a ball in her bed, letting the tears flow just as freely. Even Milton gave up on consoling her and went to sleep in the other room. Mother Nature was showing no signs of letting up today. Black clouds were overhead, drowning out the sun, and although the rain had slowed to a sprinkle, the rain was expected to return with a vengeance later that morning.

She managed a shower and got dressed, but it didn't improve her mood. She hated herself for being so soft-hearted and stupid. She might have told herself that it wouldn't happen, that they were too different, but that had been short-sighted. He was smart and hiding a very tender inside, all wrapped up in an incredible package. Of course she'd fallen. Of course.

As she walked out her front door to leave for work, she was unfortunately reminded of the other thing she didn't want to think about today—the situation with her dad. A car she didn't recognize was parked across the street, and a man was standing at the curb with his phone, taking pictures of her. She stalked to her car, hopped in and flipped him off as she drove by. Not a smart move. She didn't care.

By the time she arrived at Moonlight Ridge, walked through the parking lot, into the inn, and up to her office, she knew how much everyone on staff was talking about her. Gossiping. Despite her inclination to ignore everything, she had to see what the stories were saying. So she did the unthinkable—an internet search for her dad's name.

It was all exactly what she'd expected.

"Accused Hollywood Producer Uses Daughter as Shield."

"Leo Kincaid: 'My daughter hasn't given up on me.'"

"A Daughter's Love Comforts Controversial Producer."

The stuff people were assuming about her was mostly wrong. She didn't want to reconcile with her dad. She didn't want to be a part of his life anymore.

She hated the things he'd done. But one thing was right—somewhere in her heart, there was still a glimmer of love for her dad. She'd tried to make it go away, but she couldn't.

The worst of the stories were the few that rehashed the whole wedding-planner-left-at-the-altar story. How the media loved a good juicy twist of fate, and that was one for the ages. Of course, in the context of that particular angle came the unavoidable mention of Moonlight Ridge. She hated that she was once again the reason a negative light had been cast on the property. It wasn't fair to the Holloways. It wasn't fair to Jameson.

Autumn's phone silently buzzed, facedown on her desk. She'd put it on mute out of necessity. She was getting dozens of calls, so many that it was draining her battery, mostly from numbers she did not recognize. She was going to have to get a new number, or perhaps this was the time to cut herself off from society, move deep into the woods and live off the grid.

But something made her look at her phone. It was Delilah Barefoot. Autumn scrambled to answer, hoping to hell this was a phone call about table runners or cake toppers or something uncontroversial.

"Delilah, hi. How nice to hear from you. What can I help you with?" Autumn turned in her chair and looked out the window. Impossibly, the sky was getting even darker. The rain was coming down harder now. Lightning crackled across the sky. A few seconds later, thunder boomed so loudly the entire inn shook.

"I don't really know how to say this, so I'll just come out with it. We can't have our wedding at Moonlight

Ridge. My mother saw your dad on television. She's not happy. She wants her deposit back. I hope that will be okay."

Autumn hated how the ripple effects of this disaster were spreading. She also hated that it was ruining what should be a fun process for Delilah. "I understand. I'm so sorry that it came to this. Truly. If it'll help at all, I'm happy to help coordinate when you find a new venue."

Delilah's voice got quiet. "Moonlight Ridge isn't the issue, Autumn."

*Oh right. I'm the problem.* The realization hit her like a steamroller. She was flattened. After last night, Autumn had thought there were no more uncomfortable truths to hear. She'd been wrong. "What if I wasn't here? Like at all."

"I'm not sure. My mom is a piece of work. Plus, I don't want to make you quit your job."

"You know, this was already in the works. I'd been planning to leave," she lied. "I don't want to hurt the resort."

"I'm so sorry, Autumn. I know how hard it is to be in the shadow of a well-known parent."

"Thank you. That means a lot." Autumn choked back tears. "So please let your mom know that she doesn't need to worry about me anymore. By the time you have your wedding, no one will even remember."

"I'll try, but no promises."

"All you can do is your best."

Autumn said goodbye, not yet fully absorbing that she'd just committed to leave Moonlight Ridge and the resort still might lose a huge booking. But she didn't see another path forward. She had to leave. Even though being the wedding planner at Moonlight Ridge was her dream job, and she adored everyone there, she was hurting the place she loved. If she followed her natural inclination to look at the bright side, there was one good result from this. She wouldn't have to be reminded of Grey every time she came to work.

She pulled up a word document on her computer and typed out a letter to end her contract with Moonlight Ridge. Despite the few tears she'd shed on the phone with Delilah, there was no time spent being sentimental or crying. This was short and sweet. To the point. She hit print, scrawled her name across the bottom and then prepared herself for her next hurdle. Molly was the natural recipient of this letter, and she was not going to let Autumn leave without a fight.

Autumn walked with purpose down to Molly's office. But when she poked her head inside, Mack was there. Not Molly.

"Hey," Mack said, looking up from a three-ring binder. "How are you doing today? Grey said you weren't feeling well."

Clearly, Grey had not told his brother what had happened between them. "I'm okay. Is Molly around?"

"She's not. She's chasing down maintenance. There's a broken pipe in one of the guest rooms. I just stopped in because she asked me to look over some projections." Mack sat back in his chair. "But I'm glad you're here. I saw the story about your dad. We should probably have a chat about it and the potential fallout."

Autumn knew then that she was doing the right

thing. She took a deep breath. It was time to cut her ties with the Holloway family. She handed over the letter, then stepped back from the desk and gathered her hands behind her back. "Yeah, about that. You don't need to worry about me. I'm leaving."

Mack glanced at the letter. "I see."

"I want to thank you and your family for allowing me to work as a contractor for Moonlight Ridge. But it's time for me to go. There's no reason for you to keep me when I'm only hurting business." She swallowed hard, willing herself to not cry, and hoping like hell that Delilah Barefoot wouldn't end up canceling after all. "I'll clean out my work space immediately. I can get you a list of possible replacements for me next week."

Mack set aside the letter. "I'm sorry to hear this. Molly will be really sad to hear it, too. But I appreciate you making this sacrifice for my family. And for the resort. That means a lot right now. Truly."

Autumn merely nodded, forcing a polite smile. "No problem."

"You'll still be there for the wedding, right? Molly would lose it if you weren't there."

In the midst of all of this, Autumn had completely forgotten about Mack and Molly's wedding. Not only was Autumn the maid of honor, Grey was a groomsman. She'd be subjected to a horribly romantic day with the man she loved in close proximity. What a nightmare. "Yes. Of course. I'll be there." At least Grey would be leaving Asheville the day after, and Autumn could begin the process of starting over. Again.

Outside, lightning struck once more. The rain was

coming down in torrential sheets. The lights in the building flickered, then another loud boom of thunder came. "I'd better get going," she said, then quickly ducked out into the hall. This all seemed like a fitting ending to her stint at Moonlight Ridge—straight out of a horror movie.

Grey was trying hard to get work done, but it was pointless. He hadn't slept at all last night, haunted by the vision of Autumn walking away from him. Right out of his life. Outside, it was dark as night and it wasn't even noon. The rain was unrelenting. Grey had never liked weather like this. It was too unpredictable. He had no control. It was also a huge reminder of the night Travis went out into the storm and he and Mack had chased after him. In a split second, everything changed. Just like Jameson's brain episode had changed things again.

Maybe it was the lack of sleep, but Grey felt like he couldn't see anything clearly. Lately, Autumn had been the person in his life who'd made things make sense, but he couldn't reach out to her. She'd be furious with him. Which left Mack. Grey felt so unsettled right now and he had to do something about it. So he reached for his phone. Just as he picked it up, a screeching sound came from the device—the emergency warning system. A quick glance told him that there was flash flooding in the area. Good thing he didn't need to go anywhere.

"I was just about to call you," Mack answered. "Have you talked to Autumn?"

"Not since yesterday." Grey still hadn't told his

brother about their falling-out. "We had an argument. Or a disagreement."

"About what?"

"About me leaving. She told me she loves me."

Mack grumbled on the other end of the line. "I thought you were keeping things casual. Why didn't you stick to the plan?"

It was such a simple question, the sort of thing Grey asked himself all the time. He loved plans. His entire career revolved around them. When he made one he always stuck to it. But he hadn't with Autumn. "It just happened."

"Did you tell her you loved her, too?"

"No." He felt sick about it, but he'd been too angry about Mack trying to get him to do something he hadn't planned to.

"So you don't love her?"

Grey was about to say that he had feelings for Autumn he couldn't explain. But that wasn't entirely true. They were simple—he wanted to be with her. He wanted to protect her and keep her safe. She made him look at the whole world differently. But…he was afraid to label his feelings as love. Love could go away. It could fade or get twisted into something else. It happened with his parents. It happened with his brothers. Then again, he'd found a new parental love with Jameson. And he and his brothers were finding their way back. "Dammit, Mack. I messed everything up. I should have told her I loved her, but I panicked. Why did you have to pick that fight with me yesterday, anyway?"

"Because I love you, you big dummy. And I want you to stay here."

Grey could hardly believe he'd been so stupid. "I have to go. I have to talk to Autumn."

"She just left. She quit her job and emptied out her office."

"What? Because of me?"

"I'm sure you'd love to think that, but it was because of everything with her dad. The Barefoot family was going to cancel their wedding. She saw that it was hurting the resort."

"She can't quit."

"Too late. She already did."

"No. Let me fix this. I have to call her now. Bye."

"Hold on. Can I give you one piece of advice?"

"What?"

"Don't call her if you aren't ready to tell her that you love her."

*I know that now.* "I have to go. Bye, Mack." Grey hung up and immediately called Autumn's cell. It went straight to voice mail. He ended the call and sent her a text. Please answer your phone. He called again.

"What do you want, Grey? I don't want to talk to you right now. I'm trying to drive home through a monsoon."

"Why are you on the roads right now? There are flash flood warnings."

"I know that. I'm fine. Or maybe a river will just carry me away and nobody will need to worry about me anymore."

"I would worry about you, Autumn. I always will."

"Next subject, please." The anger in her voice was unavoidable. He had to see her. He had to tell her in person what he was feeling.

"Look, Autumn, we need to talk. Pull over to the side of the road and I'll find you. What route are you taking?"

"The back way. I figured the old logging road lets me avoid most of the low-lying areas."

Grey's heart began to pound. The mere mention of the logging road made him sick to his stomach. "But that stretch of road before the ravine. It gets washed out sometimes." The lights in Grey's cottage flickered. It felt like a bad omen.

"I'm fine. Don't—" There was a click on the line.

"Autumn? Hello?" There was no answer. Grey's mind switched into overdrive. What if she'd gone off the road? What if she was hurt? What if she was dead and he'd never get to tell her how he felt? He grabbed his keys and ran out to his car, already soaked by the time he hopped inside. For a moment, he hesitated. He knew his blood was running hot right now. Emotions were at a fever pitch. And Mother Nature was not playing nice. This was exactly what it was like the night he and Mack went out after Travis. The night when everything went horribly, horribly wrong. Was this a mistake? Was he about to do something truly stupid?

Of course, he could answer neither of those questions. This was the unknown in all of its glory and he had to face it. He had to fight through it. With his hand trembling, he stuck his key in the ignition and started the engine. He put it into gear, knowing he couldn't leave Autumn out in this. He cared too much. He loved her.

The car fishtailed when he punched the accelerator, and he nearly peeled out of the driveway next to his cottage. Luckily, there were very few cars out in this weather, so Grey was able to get to the old logging road in no time flat. His heart raced just as fast as the wipers struggled to keep up with the rain. He was pushing the speed limit, which he knew was unwise, but it was the only way he stood any chance of catching up to her. He hoped she had the sense to take things slow. Autumn's eyesight was not great, even with her glasses on. Plus, and this was the big thing—she was upset. The thought of her behind the wheel right now was too much. All he could do was focus on the road and finding her. He rounded a big curve and he knew that he wasn't far from the ravine. Up ahead, he saw fuzzy red lights. Brake lights. A car was stopped on the side of the road. A silver car.

*Autumn.* His gut instinct was to drive like a bat out of hell, but it wasn't safe, especially not in these slick conditions, so he slowed down. His heart was threatening to beat its way out of his chest as he eased up behind the car and turned off his engine. There was no sign of life in the car. Definitely no Autumn. And she'd left her headlights on, which he found odd. It hadn't been that long ago that she'd had to replace her battery.

He climbed out of his car, immediately getting soaked in a deluge of rain. The sound was deafening. Lightning crackled across the sky. He walked to the driver's side door and shielded his eyes with his hands, peering into the window. She wasn't inside. He straightened and looked down the road, but there was no sign of her. "Autumn?" he called with hands cupped around his mouth.

"Grey?" her voice was small and muffled, but it gave him life.

"Autumn? Where are you?" He turned back and that was when he saw her car rock side to side. He rounded the front to the passenger side and that was where he found her—crouched down trying to turn a nut on her tire. The relief he felt was so immediate he wondered how he could've ever doubted his feelings for her. "Autumn! You're okay."

She fell back on her butt, sitting in the muddy ditch with a tire iron in her hand. Her glasses were foggy and had slid down to the end of her nose. Her hair was just as wet as it had been when they'd gone skinny-dipping. "Grey? You came looking for me? I told you not to."

He dropped to his knees next to her, one landing in soft and muddy ground, not that he cared. He took her hand. "Of course I did. I had to go after the woman I love."

She just stared at him from behind those glasses. "What did you just say?"

"I love you. I should have said it yesterday. I was feeling it, I just hadn't wrapped my head around the idea of it. Probably because admitting my feelings for you means that I would have to stay, and that would've meant giving in to Mack's demands."

Autumn scrambled to her feet and looked down at

him, aggressively pointing at him with the tire iron. "If you're leaving, I don't want to hear that you love me."

He hurried back to standing, not bothering with the pretense of brushing himself off. He was a disaster. So was Autumn, although she managed to make it look beautiful. "I'm not leaving."

"You're not?"

He shook his head. He wanted her in his arms. "Will you put down the damn tire iron, please?"

She dropped it to the ground, her shoulders drooping in defeat.

He didn't waste a second reining her into his arms so he could hold her close and watch the water drip down the tip of her nose.

"Are you serious? Are you really not leaving?"

He nodded emphatically. "I'm staying. I love you, Autumn, and I know it's only been a few months, but I hope that you'll still want to see me. I'm hoping you can forgive me for everything that happened yesterday. I had a momentary blip of insanity."

Autumn looked straight up at the sky for a moment, letting the rain fall on her face. "I'd say that this is your blip of insanity."

"You stood in the rain for me yesterday. I figured the least I could do was get soaked for you."

"Can we put that part to a stop though? The getting wet part?"

Grey grabbed her hand. "Yes. Come on. Let's get into my car. We'll come back for yours after the storm is over." They rushed back to his rental, and he opened the passenger side for her before he climbed in on the driver's side. They were both a sight—dripping wet, muddy and looking exhausted.

"I had to quit my job today," Autumn said.

Grey started the engine. "I know. It's okay. We'll figure something out."

"I don't see how. I think that part of my life is over."

It pained Grey to hear her say that but there were only so many problems he could solve at once. He leaned over and placed a soft kiss on her lips. "Then hopefully we can start a new part of your life together."

# Thirteen

Autumn nearly cried when Molly said, "I do."

"I now pronounce you husband and wife. You may kiss the bride," the minister said.

A cacophony of hooting, hollering and applause rang out from the crowd gathered for Mack and Molly's wedding. Mack dipped Molly in one of the hottest kisses Autumn had ever witnessed. The happy couple then stood hand in hand before the friends and family assembled in the old barn, which was now mere weeks away from being the latest location of a Corkscrew Craft Beer Brewery.

Autumn sniffled, but she wasn't sad. She was overflowing with joy for the happy ending her best friend now had with the love of her life. As Mack and Molly started down the aisle together, Grey stepped forward and offered his arm.

"We have got to stop meeting like this," he said.

Autumn laughed under her breath and looped her arm in his, snugging him closer while they made their own journey to the back of the room. The old Grey didn't joke around much, but she knew now that she hadn't really known the real Grey. The one he spent a lot of years hiding from those around him.

Momentarily relieved of their wedding party duties, it was time for Autumn to spring into action. "I need to take care of a few small details."

"Always the wedding planner," Grey said.

"Miraculously, yes." Autumn planted a kiss on his cheek. "I'll come find you in a few minutes?"

"Don't be too long." Grey went to join his brother Travis, who was making his way toward the bar.

Autumn took that as her cue to get to work, taking care of the tiny tasks that make a wedding a success, like talking to the DJ and making sure the catering department started handing out champagne and hors d'oeuvres. She was so happy knowing she had her job back. Grey had done the unthinkable by stepping into the fray and saving the Barefoot wedding *and* her job. He'd done it by calling his old friend Archer. The two even went out for a beer, and according to Grey, they talked about things like falling in love with a woman you adore. By the end of the evening, Grey had convinced Archer to reframe the idea of Autumn organizing the wedding. He'd instructed Archer to tell his future mother-in-law that it wasn't fair to hold Autumn accountable for the things her father had done. Guilt by association wasn't something a US Senator should go around trying to impose. Apparently, it had worked, and all was back on track with Autumn as Moonlight Ridge's wedding planner. Thank goodness.

After she took care of a few details, she noticed Grey sitting at one of the round tables with Travis. The two were deep in conversation, so Autumn approached slowly. "I hope I'm not interrupting," she said.

"Are you kidding? Never," Grey said, pulling out a chair for her. "We were just talking about some of the things that will happen when Travis comes back to help out."

"My brothers have a big to-do list for me," Travis said.

"Oh yeah? Like what?" Autumn asked.

"Primarily helping them overhaul catering."

Autumn wasn't shocked. The reports on the food were sometimes spotty. She'd had many conversations with Molly about the menu being stuck in the past. "Will you be working with the brewery at all?"

"I don't know," Travis said. "Mack has his own menu and chefs."

Autumn couldn't help but notice that Travis seemed to have the same attitude Grey had when he'd first arrived back at Moonlight Ridge. Perhaps it was time to change the subject. "Grey, when will the brewery equipment go in?" Autumn flagged down a waiter and asked him to leave champagne for each of them.

"I need to talk to Mack about all of that, but I would

think the brewery and kitchen will be up and running in a month or two," Grey said.

Travis took a long sip of his champagne. "Autumn. I need to ask you a question."

Grey slid his brother a look. "What are you getting into, T?"

Travis reared back his head. "Do you know how long it's been since you called me T?"

Grey looked surprised, glancing back and forth between Travis and Autumn. "I guess it's been a long time, huh?"

"A very long time," Travis said.

"I didn't even think about it. It just came out of my mouth."

Travis's otherwise stern expression slowly turned to a smile, which made Autumn extremely happy. Grey and Mack had pretty well made amends, but Travis had missed out on all of that over the last few months. Hopefully his longer visit would help the brothers continue to heal the broken bonds between them. Autumn knew that it all weighed on Grey.

"Okay, well, nicknames aside, I need to ask Autumn that question," Travis said. "Is it true that my brother Grey went out in a dangerous storm looking for you?" He arched one eyebrow at Grey.

Autumn knew what Travis was getting at. Grey had told her that was a big part of what sparked the argument between the brothers the night of the accident—Travis had gone looking for a girl he had a thing for, and Mack and Grey thought he was crazy for doing it.

"It is true. And I told him not to come looking for me. He did it anyway."

"I was worried," Grey pled. "Plus, her phone died in the middle of our conversation. Anyone would have done what I did."

"And how did it turn out?" Autumn asked Grey.

"You had a flat tire and I rescued you. That's how it turned out."

She laughed quietly. "It *all* turned out fine, didn't it? I told you it would."

Grey shook his head. "She always thinks everything will be fine," he said to Travis. "But that's not always true. Sometimes things don't work out."

"Same old pessimistic Grey." Travis's phone rang and he glanced at the screen. "I hope you two will excuse me. I need to take this."

"Of course," Autumn said.

Travis got up from the table and Grey instantly took her hand. "I hope you don't think of me as pessimistic. I'm trying to be better. You make me want to be better."

She loved how sweet he was. She loved everything about him. "I know you're doing your best. And I don't want you to change entirely. The man I fell in love with is at least a little bit pessimistic. We need to be able to balance each other out."

Grey leaned over and kissed her on the cheek. "I love you, Autumn."

"I love you, too. I really, really do."

Grey pointed across the room. "Hey. Are Mack and Molly supposed to be dancing already?"

Autumn turned, and sure enough, not only were the

bride and groom slow-dancing, Giada and Jameson were doing the same. "It's their wedding." Autumn consulted her watch. "And actually, dinner won't be served for another thirty minutes."

Grey got up from the table and offered his hand. "If we have to wait a half hour, I think I should take this chance to ask for a dance."

Autumn grinned wide, feeling heat creep across her cheeks. "Sounds great."

Grey led her out to the dance floor, then pulled her into his arms as soon as they arrived. The music was soft and slow and incredibly romantic. As someone who relished the more fanciful details of a wedding, it was nice to attend one that was casual and where it was okay for a few rules to be broken.

"You know, this reminds me of that night at Mack and Molly's engagement party. When we danced and I wondered what in the heck we were doing."

Grey laughed. "I knew exactly what I was doing. I was trying to get you out of that dress you were wearing."

"It didn't take you long."

"I'm very focused when I decide what I want."

Autumn looked up at him and their gazes connected. Would she ever stop feeling so amazing when he looked at her like that? She truly hoped that she would feel like that forever. "I'm glad."

"And speaking of what I want, I need to talk to you about something." He spun her in a few circles, until they were off in a quieter corner of the dance floor.

"What exactly?"

"I know we've only been together for a few months, but I feel like what we have is pretty great."

"You'll get no argument from me on that. What's your point?"

Grey swayed her back and forth, his hand traveling all over her back, bringing every nerve ending to life. "Maybe it was seeing my brother make the leap today, but now that I'm staying in Asheville, and we know we want to be together, I guess I just feel like we should think about other steps."

Autumn wasn't quite sure where he was going with this. "Like moving in together?"

"Well, sure. Definitely that. But beyond that, I guess I want you to know that whenever you feel like you're over everything that happened, I'd like to have the chance to put a ring on your finger. I just don't want to push you before you're ready."

A soft laugh left Autumn's lips. "Are you proposing to me at your brother's wedding?"

"Only if you want me to. And don't tell Mack. He'll kill me."

Autumn wasn't quite ready for engagement, but it was so reassuring that Grey wanted to talk about it at all. "When the time is right I want a small wedding. No big production."

"So says the professional wedding planner. And you know, people say that and it always ends up being bigger."

Autumn giggled. "And I want a fancy honeymoon. Somewhere warm."

Grey nodded, trailing his hand up and down her spin,

making her dizzy with contentment. "Oh, yes. Somewhere like Bali where they have those huts out on the water and you can just dive right into the ocean."

"That sounds amazing. I've always wanted to go on a trip like that."

"As long as we go somewhere that doesn't require you to wear a lot of clothes."

"That sounds like a lot of beaches and sunshine, Grey. I thought the East Coast guy wasn't into that."

He shrugged and tugged her closer. "What can I say? You've changed me. For the better."

She nuzzled her face in his neck and kissed the sensitive spot below his ear. His warm smell sent ripples of anticipation through her. She couldn't wait until they could get back to her place, cast aside their wedding garb, and lose themselves in each other.

"I'm so glad you decided to stay in Asheville. You've made me so happy."

Grey took her for a spin, holding her tight against his warm frame. "Good. Because as long as you're happy, I will be, too."

"You really love me, don't you?"

"I do."

\* \* \* \* \*

*Look for the next book in the Moonlight Ridge trilogy.*

**Just a Little Married**
*by Reese Ryan*

*Available next month!*

# WE HOPE YOU ENJOYED
## THIS BOOK FROM

### ⬡ HARLEQUIN
# DESIRE

*Luxury, scandal, desire—welcome to
the lives of the American elite.*

Be transported to the worlds of oil barons, family dynasties,
moguls and celebrities. Get ready for juicy plot twists,
delicious sensuality and intriguing scandal.

**6 NEW BOOKS AVAILABLE EVERY MONTH!**

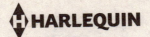

## #2827 RANCHER'S CHRISTMAS STORM
*Gold Valley Vineyards* • by Maisey Yates

Things have been tense since rancher Jericho Smith's most recent acquisition—Honey Cooper's family winery. What she thought was her inheritance now belongs to her brother's infuriatingly handsome best friend. But when they're forced together during a snowstorm, there's no escaping the heat between them...

## #2828 BIDDING ON A TEXAN
*Texas Cattleman's Club: Heir Apparent*
by Barbara Dunlop

To save their families' reputations and fortunes, heiress Gina Edmonds and hardworking business owner Rafe Cortez-Williams reluctantly team up for a cowboy bachelor auction. Their time together reveals an undeniable attraction, but old secrets may derail everything they hope to build...

## #2829 THE EX UPSTAIRS
*Dynasties: The Carey Center* • by Maureen Child

A decade ago, Henry Porter spent one hot night with Amanda Carey before parting on bad terms. They're both powerful executives now, and he's intentionally bought property she needs. To find out why, Amanda goes undercover as his new maid, only to be tempted by him again...

## #2830 JUST A LITTLE MARRIED
*Moonlight Ridge* • by Reese Ryan

To claim her inheritance, philanthropist Riley George makes a marriage deal with the celebrity chef catering her gala, Travis Holloway—who's also her ex. Needing the capital for his family's resort, Travis agrees. It's strictly business until renewed sparks and long-held secrets threaten everything...

## #2831 A VERY INTIMATE TAKEOVER
*Devereaux Inc.* • by LaQuette

Once looking to take him down, Trey Devereaux must now band together with rival Jeremiah Benton against an even larger corporate threat. But as tensions grow, so does the fire between them. When secrets come to light, can they save the company *and* their relationship?

## #2832 WHAT HAPPENS AT CHRISTMAS...
*Clashing Birthrights* • by Yvonne Lindsay

As CEO Kristin Richmond recovers from a scandal that rocked her family's business, a new threat forces her to work with attorney Hudson Jones, who just happens to be the ex who left her brokenhearted. But Christmas brings people together...especially when there's chemistry!

---

SPECIAL EXCERPT FROM

**H**HARLEQUIN

# DESIRE

*Things have been tense since rancher Jericho Smith's
most recent acquisition—Honey Cooper's family winery.
What she thought was her inheritance now belongs
to her brother's ridiculously handsome best friend.
But when they're forced together during a snowstorm,
there's no escaping the heat between them...*

*Read on for a sneak peek at*
Rancher's Christmas Storm
*by* New York Times *bestselling author Maisey Yates!*

"Maybe you could stay." Her voice felt scratchy; she
felt scratchy. Her heart was pounding so hard she could
barely hear, and the steam filling up the room seemed to
swallow her voice.

But she could see Jericho's face. She could see the
tightness there. The intensity.

"Honey..."

"No. I just... Maybe this is the time to have a
conversation, actually. The one that we decided to have
later. Because I'm getting warm. I'm very warm."

"Put your robe back on."

"What if I don't want to?"

"Why not?"

"Because I want you. I already admitted to that. Why
do you think I'm so upset? All the time? About all the
women that you bring into the winery, about the fact that

my father gave it to you. About the fact that we're stuck together, but will never actually be together. And that's why I had to leave. I'm not an idiot, Jericho. I know that you and I are never going to… We're not going to fall in love and get married. We can hardly stand to be in the same room as each other.

"But I have wanted you since I understood what that meant. And I don't know what to do about it. Short of running away and having sex with someone else. That was my game plan. My game plan was to go off and have sex with another man. And that got thwarted. You were the one that picked me up. You're the one that I'm stuck here with in the snow. And I'm not going to claim that it's fate. Because I can feel myself twisting every single element of this except for the weather. The blizzard isn't my fault. But I'm making the choice to go ahead and offer…me."

"I…"

"If you're going to reject me, just don't do it horribly."

And then suddenly she found herself being tugged into his arms, the heat from his body more intense than the heat from the sauna, the roughness of his clothes a shock against her skin. And then his mouth crashed down on hers.

*Don't miss what happens next in…*
Rancher's Christmas Storm
*by* New York Times *bestselling author Maisey Yates!*

*Available October 2021 wherever*
*Harlequin Desire books and ebooks are sold.*

Harlequin.com

HDEXP0921